When Giraffes Flew

Jeff Weddle

Published by:
Southern Yellow Pine (SYP) Publishing, LLC
4351 Natural Bridge Rd.
Tallahassee, FL 32305

www.syppublishing.com

This is a work of fiction. Names, characters, places, and events that occur either are the products of the author's imagination or are used fictitiously. Any resemblance to actual persons, places, or events is purely co-incidental.

The contents and opinions expressed in this book do not necessarily reflect the views and opinions of Southern Yellow Pine Publishing, nor does the mention of brands or trade names constitute endorsement.

ISBN-10: 1940869609
ISBN-13: 978-1-940869-60-5
ISBN-13: 978-1-940869-58-2 ePub
ISBN-13: 978-1-940869-59-9 Adobe PDF eBook
Library of Congress Control Number: 2015952847

Cover Design: Jim Hamer

Printed in the United States of America
First Edition October 2015

Acknowledgements

Grateful acknowledgment is made to the publications in which some of these stories first appeared.

ArtMag; *Black Heart Magazine*; *Chiron Review*; *Fiction on the Web*; *Fictionvale*; *Free Flash Fiction*; *Inscape*; *Journal of Kentucky Studies*; *Midday Moon*; *Out of the Gutter Online*; *Port Cities Review*; *Pressure Press Presents*; *Prime Number Magazine*; *Red Fez*; *Roadside Fiction*; *Surreal South '13*; *Thrice Fiction*

Dedication

Always for Jill

Contents

A Feast of Feathers

You're ten years old the day the chickens explode. What could possibly prepare you for this? You're in the living room watching TV, and you hear the bang out in the yard, and you run to the door. A pickup truck is turned over beside a broken elm tree, and there are chicken crates everywhere and chickens all over the yard. Some of the chickens look dead already, but others are screaming and running around flapping their wings. Poochie and Smoke appear from somewhere out back and lay in on the chickens. They bite the heads and sling the bodies, both just the same, as if they had been taught to do this. They kill the birds and eat their fill, then kill more and leave them lying dead on the lawn.

"Mama," you scream, but she's not there. She's visiting her sister in town, and you're in the house alone—just you and the wrecked truck in the yard and all those chickens. Dead chickens, dying chickens, chickens being murdered by the dogs. The scene is horrible. Poochie and Smoke fight over a small bird. Poochie has it by the head and Smoke has a wing. The wing rips off, and Poochie backs away, growling.

"Mama," you scream again.

The driver is still in the truck, but you don't know this. You don't even think about him. All you can think about is the chickens in your front yard.

You don't know how long it is before you think to call somebody. You call your mother at your aunt's house and tell her what's happening.

"Calm down," she says. "Talk slow. Tell me what's the matter."

Where do you start? What can you tell her?

"Feathers," you say. "There are all these feathers. The yard is filled with them."

"Feathers?"

But that's all you can think to say. After a while, she stops trying to get the story, and says she's coming right home. You hang up but don't dare walk back to the door. Instead, you go back and stare at the television. You turn up the sound so you can't hear what's going on outside.

The front door opens. There's a man standing there, a man you don't know. He's bloody and feathers are stuck all over him. He looks like a big, awful rooster. He stands there in your front room for a second then dips over and slides against the wall, all the way to the floor. There's a wide trail of blood where he slides. You realize this isn't good.

This is the driver. He's a farmer from out in the county, and he was on his way to sell his chickens in town. Now he's had a bad experience in your yard, and his chickens are mostly beyond salvage. Now he's lying on your living room floor bleeding to death, feathers stuck all over his body. Now you have to deal with him.

But of course you can't. There's nothing to do but sit where you are and wait. The noise outside has quieted to the din of a few dozen chickens clucking and squawking. The dogs have followed the man into the house. This is the biggest chicken of them all, and they each know they must have him. Smoke wises up and latches onto his head, just above the cheek, and locks her jaw tight. Poochie has a shoulder. They try their best to sling him around and kill him, but he weighs too much. They growl and jerk, but it's no good.

You run over and kick the dogs away, but they are crazed with blood. For a moment it looks like they're going to jump on

2

you, but they don't; they want the big chicken and nothing is going to keep them from having it.

By the time your mother arrives it's all over. The man's face and arm are chewed to pieces. He's on the floor, dead—blood and feathers stuck all over the floor and walls.

Your mother doesn't know what to make of any of this. You think she'll scream or faint, but what she does is scoop you up and run into the bathroom and lock the door.

"Are you okay?" she yells at you. "Are you okay?"

There is no way to answer this question. You sit on her lap and shake your head back and forth, but you don't know what you're doing.

A week later, things are mostly back to normal. The truck has been towed away and most of the feathers are gone from the yard. The front room is immaculate. The broken elm tree has been removed. A man from the sheriff's office has come and taken Smoke and Poochie away. You cried over the dogs.

When the deputy came for them, you tried to keep him away, but you've learned now, there's no fighting a man with a badge and a gun.

Your mother hasn't left your side in seven days.

"Mama," you tell her, "the chicken man can't hurt us anymore."

She smiles the tiniest bit, but you know she believes something different. From now on, every so often, the yard will yield a host of bones.

If there is anything in the world you miss more than your dogs, you don't want to think of it. At night, now, you wonder about all that road out there. There must be more trucks heading your way, and maybe chickens aren't the worst of it. It's hard to imagine this might be true, but something tells you to believe it.

Hot Sardines

Marge and Fran were in the BeeQuick shopping for sardines. It was Friday noon, and Marge's son, Buddy, was supposed to be home about five thirty. Buddy loved sardines, and he didn't get to eat any while he was in jail, so Marge wanted to make sure there were some at the house when he got there.

Fran picked up a can of fancy herring parts in soybean oil. "How about these?"

Marge looked the can over. "No, he doesn't like those. He likes the ones in Cajun hot sauce." Fran put the fancy herring parts back on the shelf.

"Well, I don't see any of that kind here. I guess we'd better go someplace else."

"Guess so. But I need to get home pretty quick and clean up the trailer. I want it all perfect when Buddy gets home."

Fran nodded. She knew Marge was hinting that maybe Fran could do her a little favor by going into town and picking up some hot sardines while Marge went home and cleaned up for Buddy's homecoming. They stood there for a moment in silence; then Fran said, "Maybe I should go get the sardines while you go home and get ready."

"Oh, could you? That would just save me." Marge's eyes got big and round, and her smile showed all her teeth.

"Sure, Marge. Glad to." They walked outside and got into Marge's car and drove back to the trailer Marge shared with Buddy—when he was home. Fran got into her old Volkswagen and was pulling away when Marge yelled at her, "Remember—Cajun hot sauce! Get three cans!"

Fran stuck her hand out the window and waved, then drove off. Marge went inside and sat down on the couch. There was a bottle of gin on the coffee table and a revolver. They both belonged to Buddy. She opened the gin and took a little sip. Awful! How could Buddy drink that stuff? It was gin that caused all the trouble, too. Buddy and a couple of boys he worked with down at the dairy got all liquored up and messed with that trashy Hoage girl. The girl said they took liberties. The boys said it was a lie, and of course it was; but the judge took the girl's word, and now all three of the boys were charged with harassment. At least there was that. At least they amended the charge down to harassment. They were good boys, after all, and everyone knew about the Hoages. Why, old Marcus Hoage hadn't worked an honest day in twenty years. Marge knew the kind, always looking for a way to beat honest folks out of something. If little Dorey went for a ride, it was pretty clear that she was looking for a good time. Sure, the boys were looking for some fun, too. And why not? And what was wrong with that?

Meanwhile, Fran was on her way to Kroger to look for Buddy's Cajun hot sardines. Hot sardines, indeed. What that Buddy needed was a can of hot sardines shoved up his butt. Fran didn't know Dorey Hoage, but she did know Buddy and those thugs he hung with at work. They were the type who'd force a girl to do something she didn't want to. Boy, were they. Fran and Marge had been friends since grade school, and they talked about everything. But Marge didn't know about the time Fran was down at Ireland's and got hooked up with Buddy and his friends. It wasn't too long after her divorce, and she was lonesome. Buddy was just a kid, as far as Fran was concerned. Right. She had enough sense not to get into a car with them, but they were all over her, right there in the bar. She said okay to a game of pool, and midway through the game, little Jimmy Robinson had his hands on her. Fran didn't think much about it at first. In fact, it was kind of nice, but here she was, old enough to be, well, old enough to be their aunt, and it just wasn't right. After the game the boys let her go back to her table without any trouble, though for a minute, it looked like she would have to slap Buddy just to keep him from pawing her.

Fran was about to turn into the Kroger parking lot when Marcus Hoage passed her heading back the other way. Fran didn't know Marcus, but she noted the weathered, black Buick as it cruised by. It swerved almost into her lane to miss the split carcass of a large dog that lay in the middle of the road.

"Asshole," Fran said out loud. Then she turned her car toward Kroger in search of three cans of Cajun hot sardines. The parking lot was packed. Fran circled the lot three times before she found a parking place. Finally, a green Subaru was backing out of a spot beside the shopping-cart corral and Fran sat and waited, tapping her fingers on the steering wheel. The Subaru backed toward her, so she was blocked when an orange Cadillac pulled around end of the lane and slid into the space. By the time the Subaru was gone, the Cadillac was parked, and its driver was already squirming out of her car. The woman was enormous, three hundred fifty pounds easy. She had on a too-tight, floral print dress which made her look even fatter. Fran considered running her down as she walked past, never even glancing at Fran or her homeless Volkswagen. It took Fran five more minutes to find another spot.

"Sardines," she muttered. "Hot fucking Cajun sardines."

***

Marcus Hoage had been drinking since the early morning. It was only beer, and only Schlitz at that, so he knew he couldn't be drunk. But he also knew it was time he paid a visit to the son of a bitch who had raped his daughter. Or at least who'd tried. Dorey wasn't much. He knew that. But she was no whore. What she was was a silly little bitch who didn't have any more sense than to get into a car with a bunch of drunk goomers and go riding around with them. Buddy Wallace was the ring leader; he'd managed to get that out of her. Thank God her mother wasn't around to see this. She'd left years ago, took off with that traveling brush salesman from Alabama. But Doreen, Dorey's mother, had spunk to her. If she'd still been around, there likely would be somebody dead about now, and Marcus wasn't sure if he'd be willing to take bets on which specific person that might be.

He'd heard through the grapevine—the grapevine being Teddy Stevens down at the courthouse—that Buddy Wallace was getting out of jail that afternoon, and Marcus wanted to talk to him, just talk, just to make sure he wasn't going to be bothering Dorey any more. Boys like the Wallace kid and those others— Marcus didn't put it past boys like that to try and intimidate his girl into telling the cops that she'd been mistaken about what had happened in that car down on Hawker Knob. Just end it that way. Hell, he didn't even much care if the trial didn't come to anything. Mostly he just wanted Dorey to be okay and everything back the way it was. Marcus didn't need any peckerheads trying to complicate things for him or his family just to save their own sorry skins.

Marcus popped another beer. "To Doreen, where ever you are," he said. Marcus drank a big gulp of Schlitz. He knew Buddy lived with his mother in a trailer out on Highway 4, but he wasn't sure exactly where. He was on the lookout for a green, seventy-eight Chrysler LeBaron parked in front of a beige double-wide with a redwood porch. That's all Teddy had told him.

"I sure do hate this," Marcus said to himself. It seemed like he was always having to get after some boy Dorey was fooling around with. There was that Whitaker goomer, the city councilman's son. When Marcus found Dorey and him down in the barn, Marcus was mad enough to kill. It was a good thing he didn't come in a few minutes earlier, that he didn't actually catch

7

them doing it. Then there would have been some blood gushing somewhere.

It was nothing but justice to make the boy give him that hundred dollars. It was sure better than killing him. Nobody wins when there's killing. Besides, Dorey wasn't worth that. She wasn't a whore, but she wasn't worth killing over, either. Marcus took a big swallow of beer. Like mother, like daughter. Absolutely. Doreen liked to fool around with the boys, too. That brush salesman had been coming around on his regular route for three years before Doreen ran off with him. Marcus noticed all the new brushes around the house and kept wondering how Doreen could afford such stuff. Or why she'd even want it. The hairbrushes, sure, but those others, the furniture brushes and such, it struck him as funny right off. The house was the best he could do for his family, but it wasn't exactly a showplace. Maybe some good lumber and hammers and nails might fix things up, but fancy brushes just wouldn't do the job.

Then there was that day when he came home early and saw the brush truck parked outside his house. He was still working at the ice plant in those days, and he usually worked until six o'clock. That day the compressor blew a gasket, and they shut down early. Marcus wasn't the romantic type, but he decided to bring Doreen a little gift. He stopped at the drugstore and got her a tin of rock candy, her favorite.

He had the candy in his hand when he went into the house. There they sat, Doreen and the brush man. People talked about Doreen and the brush man. It was a small town, and Marcus had heard the whispers, even though he pretended he hadn't. Marcus felt tight in his shoulders as he walked into the house, the rock candy held tightly in his hand. They were in the living room, looking at brushes. Doreen had made coffee, and they were drinking coffee and talking about brushes.

That salesman was a pretty boy, a little guy with wavy blonde hair and big eyes. He almost looked like a girl. Marcus came in, and they stopped talking and looked up at him. He felt like an idiot.

"Here." He handed Doreen the candy.

"Thanks," she said. Doreen put the tin on the floor beside her chair and looked over at the brush man. "Well, I guess I won't take anything today. Thanks so much for coming by." Marcus pretended not to be looking. Out of the corner of his eye he saw her smile at the other man. It was a pretty smile and it made him angry. It was the kind of smile that looked like it wanted to be a wink.

Marcus walked into the kitchen and sat down at the table. In a minute he heard the front door open and then shut. He heard Doreen shuffling around in the living room.

"The compressor busted. They let us go home." His voice sounded off hand, he thought. She stuck her head in the doorway.

"Oh. Are you hungry?"

Marcus nodded. "Yes, I could eat."

Doreen walked into the kitchen. She was carrying the tin of rock candy, and she put it on top of the refrigerator when she got the pork chops out.

"Let's have a good dinner," she said. "I think we should."

They were quiet through dinner. Doreen must have bought all the brushes she could use because that was the last time Marcus ever saw the brush man around his house. The Hoage house just vanished from his list. That was also the year that Dorey was born. Doreen hadn't said anything about being pregnant yet, but it was less than nine months after the day the compressor went down that Dorey came along. It cost a hundred dollars to deliver the baby at home. Dr. Burgess came over and performed the delivery.

It was funny, though. Doreen didn't fawn over her blonde baby the way it seemed mothers were supposed to. She nursed her and changed diapers, but it seemed to Marcus that his wife suffered the little girl more than she loved her. Dorey was only six months old when Doreen ran off. Marcus came in from work and found Dorey in her crib and a note lying on the kitchen table.

"Marcus,
I have left you.
Doreen"

And that's how Marcus ended up raising Dorey by himself. He found out pretty easily whom Doreen had left him for. She'd told some of the women who'd told some other women who told some men. The way they told it, she'd been messing around with the brush man for a long time. Well screw them, and screw Doreen and the brush man, too.

But that was a long time ago. All he wanted now was to find the place where Buddy Wallace and his mama lived. He just wanted to talk to them. He was reasonable. Nobody wanted any more trouble. All he wanted was for things to be okay—and maybe a little bit of compensation for swallowing his pride. What's a hundred dollars to pay for a little pride, and to make sure things worked out okay for everybody in the courts? Marcus remembered Marge Wallace. She was a pretty good woman, to his mind.

He was thinking about Marge when his tire blew. It was the rear, passenger-side tire, and it blew just as Marcus pulled out of a sharp curve and into a straight stretch. He pulled off and wrestled the spare and the jack out of the trunk. Marcus was still working on the tire when Fran, armed with three cans of hot sardines, pulled out of the Kroger parking lot and headed back toward Marge's trailer. Marcus was just about a quarter mile ahead of Fran when he got the tire changed and pulled his car back onto the road

In the trailer, a mile up the road from where Marcus's tire had blown, Marge was on her third drink. She'd decided to give the gin another try, just to see why Buddy liked it so much. It wasn't bad after the first bit, especially cut with orange juice. She took a big drink from her glass and picked up the revolver. She couldn't understand the gun, but the gin was making a lot of sense. She relaxed into the moment, thought about how good things were going to be in just a couple of hours when Buddy was back home with his mama. She heard a car pull into the driveway and then a door slam. Great, Fran was back with the sardines. There was a knock at the door.

"It's open," she said. "Come in." She lay back on the couch and pointed the gun at the door. Fran would jump a mile when she saw the gun pointed at her. It would be a big whoop for certain.

Marcus turned the knob and opened the door. He pushed it open in front of him and stepped inside quickly. Marge saw right away that it wasn't Fran. It was a man about her own age, big and ragged. A burglar? A rapist? She squeezed the trigger. Marcus jumped backward and fell onto the porch. Marge spilled half her drink on the couch as she scrambled to her feet. She set what was left in the glass on the coffee table.

"God damn it, lady. You told me to come in!"

She dropped the gun onto the wet couch and hurried to the door. Marcus was flat on his back, a growing red stain on the lower right side of his shirt. They stared at each other for a second. The man was familiar, but Marge couldn't quite place him. Marge ducked inside and picked up what was left of her drink and finished it in one gulp.

"A fine looking woman," Marcus thought to himself. "And she shot me." Marge stood over Marcus, her mouth moving but no words coming out. The telephone was in the living room and Marge was about to go inside and call 911, but the phone started ringing. She went inside to answer it, just as Fran pulled into the driveway.

"Hello?" Marge said into the receiver. "Oh, hello Buddy. You're where?"

Fran pulled in behind Marcus's car, but the redwood rail blocked her view, so she didn't see the man lying on the porch.

She had the sardines, but Kroger only had them in hot mustard, not Cajun. The whole store was crazy—people everywhere—and now she had an awful headache. She got out of her car, carrying the small, plastic bag of sardine cans. She walked three paces and saw Marcus, just as Marge was coming out the door. Marcus lay flat and still. Fran had been about to yell inside that Kroger didn't have the right kind of sardines but that Buddy better damn well like the ones she got.

"That was Buddy. Buddy just called," Marge said. "He won't be here for a while. Dorey Hoage picked him up at the jail and they're going out riding." That was the last thing Marcus heard in the world before the dark swallowed him up. Fran stood there with the sardine cans light in the bag, staring. Then Marge said, "Oh, damn it Franny, something bad's happened here, something awful. Thank God you're back—and you found the sardines!"

Dooley's Revenge

I'm in the chair for a shave when Dooley comes into the shop, plops down, and gives Lewis the eye. It was expected, sure, that Dooley would come back for his revenge, but you always hope something like that won't happen while the man who's about to be whipped is holding a razor to your throat.

"Lewis," says Dooley, "you best put away that blade before somebody gets sliced."

I nod my agreement and hope Lewis sees things that way, too.

"Tarnation," says Lewis.

"Do it," says I.

"It's for the best," says Dooley.

It's the oldest story there is: Two barbers and one majorette, the men partners before the catastrophe.

"Squeegy never loved you, Dooley," says Lewis, trembling the razor on my throat. "To tell the truth, she never loved me, either. We were used, man."

The room is quiet as forgotten pompons. Dooley shifts in his chair. There's murder in his eye, but he doesn't break for Lewis, and I'm grateful for that.

"She was mine, you whelp," says Dooley. "Who did she want to wash her hair? Who spent hours teaching her the fire baton?"

"Lies," says Lewis. It sounds like the man is crying, but I don't dare turn to look. "And who do you think taught her to tumble? Me! Me!"

Lewis sniffles and drops the razor an inch.

"Anyhow, she's gone. She ran off with old Tubbs Malloy, the fry cook at the Dairy Freeze. Tubbs always had a way with the ladies, and he plays a mean clarinet."

"Lewis," says Dooley, "don't none of it matter to me. I heard Squeegy left you in the dust. Bad luck. I just wanted to tell you about my new honey pie. Her name's Cupid LaRue, and gymnastics is her thing. I'll make her a star."

Dooley sneers as he walks out the door.

"We'll finish the shave another time," says I, pushing Lewis's hand away and rising from the chair.

"Don't anybody understand loyalty no more?" says Lewis, the tears finally gushing.

Some things a man can't never hold. Poor old Lewis.

Tubbs Malloy will fare no better. I'm the man who sewed Squeegy's first sequins, so who knows better than I? I'll see the lot of them at the next pep rally, Lewis and Dooley and Tubbs and the rest, and we'll all cheer and holler and only the strongest men will weep.

Dog Day

The telephone rang for the sixth time that hot morning, and it was still more than an hour before noon. Martin rolled onto his stomach and put the pillow over his head, but it was no use; he could still hear the rings. He lay in bed counting: seven, eight, nine, ten. The telephone rang a dozen times before Jenny hung up. He knew it was Jenny. No one else would be calling.

Martin knew Jenny was calling to find out where he was. Today was Saturday, and he was supposed to have picked up the kids at nine sharp. Jenny was calling to find out why he wasn't there. Martin didn't pick up the phone because he didn't know how to answer the question.

He had awakened at six, the clock radio blasting Steppenwolf on the oldies station. *Magic Carpet Ride*. He shut off the radio and lay still. It was so hot. He sprawled on his damp sheets for an hour, staring at the ceiling. It was early, and he knew he still had time to get up and shower and dress and pick up the kids. No problem. Then he lay there another hour, staring at the wall. And then another. At ten till nine he looked at the clock, and he knew for certain he wasn't going to make it.

At nine fifteen the phone rang for the first time. He knew it was Jenny, and he had no idea what he would say to her, so he didn't answer it. Maybe she would figure something came up and realize he wouldn't be able to come today and leave it at that. That's what Martin hoped. The phone rang again twenty minutes later and it had kept ringing every fifteen minutes or so right up till now with Martin lying on the bed, sweating, trying to shut out the rings with his pillow.

When the telephone was quiet again, Martin sat up. He looked around the room and saw the things he saw every day, the same oyster shell walls, the same red curtains, the same dresser, and the same closet doors. The same shadows moving slowly around the room.

He slung his legs across the bed and touched his feet to the floor. He walked into the kitchen and got a drink of water in a dirty coffee cup, then walked back into the bedroom and pulled open the red curtains. Sunlight hit his eyes, and Martin blinked hard, then looked out at the day. The world was a blue sky with faint, white clouds hanging in it. Below, was a street filled with cars and sidewalks thick with people. He stood there for a minute then dropped his hand and let the curtains close. He walked into the bathroom, emptied his bladder, and stepped into the shower. He let the water run over him for almost ten minutes before he washed himself.

After the shower, Martin considered going back to bed. Instead he dressed and left his apartment. It was mid-summer, and for two weeks the temperature hadn't been under ninety, day or night. Martin was already sweating by the time he made it to the corner. He looked at the time and temperature display at the bank across the street. Ninety six degrees at eleven fifty-eight a.m.

"Jesus," Martin muttered. "Hot."

He crossed the street and kept going in a straight line, block after block. He was amazed at the number of cars on the street. So much traffic. He had no destination in mind, but when he had walked six and a half blocks, he found himself in front of a pet store. Martin used his hand to shield the sun's glare on the window and look inside. He looked like he was saluting the puppies that lay on a blanket, caged just inside the window.

A small black ball of fur looked back. Martin tapped the glass and pursed his lips at the pup. Then he opened the front

16

door and walked in. It was at least ten degrees cooler inside, maybe more. Martin took a deep breath and shivered. A fat, bald man in a bright-green apron stood behind a counter, just inside the door. The fat man wiped sweat from his forehead. He was watching Martin.

"Hi there," said the fat man. "Sure is hot."

"Feels pretty good in here, though."

The fat man shrugged. "It's a matter of degrees," he said. "Get it?" The fat man laughed at his own joke. He stood there laughing so hard his belly shook. Martin tried to smile, but it came off more like a grimace. They stood there for a moment not speaking.

"How much are your puppies?" Martin finally asked.

"Those over there?" The fat man wiped tears from his eyes. "Those dogs are three-quarters shepherd. They're twenty dollars each. Quite a bargain."

"I guess."

Martin stood there for another moment, he and the fat man looking at each other. Martin shifted his weight from his left foot to his right.

"I want one," he said.

"Great. A present for the kids?"

"Sort of." He walked over to where the puppies were caged and pointed to the little black puppy lying off to the side. "I want that one," he said.

The fat man opened the cage and pulled out the pup and put it in a cardboard pet carrier. Martin dug into his wallet to pay for the dog. With tax it came to twenty-one dollars and sixty cents.

"Hope your kids will be happy with that one."

"Thanks. How'd you know I have kids?"

"Who doesn't have kids?"

Martin picked up the pet carrier and walked outside. He didn't want to go home just yet. There was a theater a couple of blocks further down the street, and he headed that way. He was pretty sure there'd be a one o'clock showing, probably for a

17

couple of bucks. He had no idea what was playing, but he knew the theater was air conditioned. Martin didn't care what was on if he could sit in the cool dark for a couple of hours.

His shirt was drenched in sweat as he fumbled for his wallet at the ticket window and tried to buy admission.

"What's in the box?" asked the old lady in the window.

"Nothing. A dog. I just bought a dog."

"No dogs."

"What?"

"No dogs allowed."

Martin didn't argue. He wanted to go in, but he knew there was no way the old bat would let him take the puppy inside. Still, it was so miserable, the weather, he was reluctant to go back to the apartment. Surely there was something he could do, someplace he could go and escape the heat. There was an ice cream shop a little farther on. That sounded good. Maybe a banana split. Maybe a milkshake. The place was bound to be air conditioned. Otherwise, how would they keep the ice cream from melting?

Martin headed for the ice cream shop. The place was busy, packed with people trying to escape the heat. It was cool, almost cold, inside. Martin waited in line for five minutes before the girl behind the counter got to him. The girl was dark and pretty and Martin enjoyed standing there in the cool store, watching her work.

"Help you?"

He wanted a strawberry milkshake. The girl made his shake, took his money and was on to the next customer. Martin took his milkshake to a table in the corner and sat and drank it. For the first time in maybe twenty minutes he thought of the dog, actually considered it sitting there in the box. Martin opened the box and looked at the puppy. It was lying on its side, staring at the wall of the box. Martin reached in and rubbed its belly and the dog wagged its tail. It didn't move around much but otherwise seemed okay. Martin closed the box.

He finished his milkshake and thought of ordering something else, just to have an excuse to stay in the shop, but he didn't. Instead he sighed and picked up the pet carrier and walked out the door. He took one last look at the girl behind the counter. She reminded him of Jenny, but then all women reminded him of Jenny these days. Of course this girl was young. Maybe that's what Donna would look like in a few years. He winced and walked out the door.

Martin trudged back the way he had come, all the way back to his building. He went inside and down the hall to his apartment. There was a note, folded in two and tacked on the door. He set the pet carrier on the floor and took the note down, unfolded it and read.

"Bastard," it said. "Where the hell are you? How could you forget your children?"

Martin folded the note and stuck it in his pocket. He unlocked the door and picked up the pet carrier and went inside. After he'd locked himself in, Martin went into the living room and opened the pet carrier and picked up the puppy. It whined and tried to squirm out of his hands, but not too much. It didn't squirm as much as Martin thought it might. Must be the heat, he figured.

"Good boy," Martin said. "Are you a good boy?" He felt stupid for buying the dog. He didn't even know why he had done it. Martin hadn't had a pet since he was nine, and his cat, Spunky, died when Martin's father backed over him in the driveway. Spunky liked to lie in the driveway and soak up the sun. Usually Martin's folks were careful about it, but one day his father forgot to look and Spunky was finished.

After that, Martin didn't want another pet. His parents offered to get him another cat or maybe a dog, but he didn't want either. The family never had another animal.

Jenny, however, had wanted a cat. She always wanted a cat, but Martin was against it. Sometimes he thought that's why Jenny ended up pregnant the first time, so she could finally have a pet,

19

even if it was a baby instead of a cat. Jenny did, in fact, mostly stop talking about a cat after Donna was born. And after Jeremy came along, Martin couldn't remember her ever mentioning animals again. He used to think that was strange. Martin kept expecting Jenny to bring up getting a pet for the kids, but that never happened.

Martin put the dog back into his box and went into the kitchen. He was thirsty but there was nothing in the refrigerator to drink. It was either lukewarm tap water or hot coffee. Martin decided on coffee. He brewed a pot, poured himself a cup and walked back into the living room. The air conditioner was broken, had been all summer, and it was so hot, but Martin drank coffee anyway. He drank his first cup, then he had another, and then one more. The puppy sat in his cardboard box and made a low whine.

After the third cup Martin picked up the phone and dialed Jenny's number. The receiver was slick in his hand. He listened to ten rings and hung up. He figured Jenny had taken the kids over to Greg's place when she realized he wasn't coming. Martin was pretty sure Jenny had planned to spend the day at Greg's place, and now she would probably be there with the kids.

He sat there for another minute, then went into the kitchen and poured another cup of coffee. It actually felt good to be drinking hot coffee on a hot day. It felt good in his throat. It also cleared away the last dregs of strawberry milkshake. It was uncomfortable having the sick, sweet, thick taste of strawberry and sugar lingering in his mouth and throat. It was too hot for it.

Martin rinsed his cup in the sink and walked into the living room. The puppy was lying on its side, eyes closed. Its breathing was rapid and shallow. Martin reached into the box and stroked the dog. It didn't do anything but lie there and breathe.

"This heat isn't good for you, is it?" Martin said. It occurred to him that maybe the puppy was dying. Maybe it was just too hot for the little dog to make it. Hell, it was almost too hot for a man to make it, let alone a little dog. Jenny, he knew, had air

20

conditioning, and so did Greg. It had been a while since Martin had seen Greg. Maybe things would be smoother now. Anyway, Martin wanted to see Jenny, and he still wanted to get his kids. So he was a few hours late. So what? Maybe the kids would even like having a dog.

He closed up the pet carrier, made sure the top was fastened tight, picked it up and left his apartment. His car was parked out back and he got inside and turned his key in the ignition. It started up, and he backed onto the street.

Greg lived halfway across town. Martin knew where he lived because, back in the old days, he and Greg had been friends. They met at work and struck up a conversation. Sometimes they ate together in the cafeteria and once in a while had a couple of beers at Lynagh's Tavern after work. They weren't good friends, but they were friends, and once or twice Martin and Jenny visited Greg and his girlfriend, Debby, at Greg's house. They'd gone over a couple of times and grilled burgers in the back yard. Martin lost track of Greg after the company downsized and laid Greg off. He heard that Greg had gotten a job with the post office after that, but he didn't hear much else.

But there sure was more. Somewhere along the way something began between Greg and Jenny, and now Jenny and Martin were divorced, and Jenny was probably over at Greg's right now with Martin's children. Martin wondered sometimes what had become of Debby.

Martin drove across town to Greg's place. Greg lived across the street from a 7-Eleven, and Martin parked in their lot. Jenny's car was on the street, right in front of Greg's house. Martin grabbed the cardboard pet carrier and got out of his car. The puppy wasn't whining or moving around. He put the box on the hood and ran his hand around the inside waist of his pants, making sure his shirt was tucked in. He smoothed back his hair, picked up the box and walked across the street. His whole body was wet with sweat.

Greg had a nice place, a ranch style house with a big picture window in the front room. Martin remembered that once he and Greg had stood looking through that window, watching Jenny and Debby sunning themselves in the yard. Martin had kept his eyes on Debby. He tried not to be obvious, to not let Greg know he was looking at his girl. He figured, now, that Greg was probably watching Jenny.

No big deal. The world didn't stop spinning. It was little things like that that bothered Martin, though. Like when Greg had the house done up in vinyl siding a couple of years ago. Martin remembered when he got the siding put on. Greg kept talking about it like it was something. "Vinyl this, vinyl that." It was just vinyl, for God's sake.

The yard was surrounded by a chain link fence, probably, Martin figured, to keep neighbor kids away from the vinyl. Martin opened the gate and walked inside. There was a cement walk from the sidewalk to the door, cutting straight through the newly mowed grass. Greg had a rock garden going on either side of the walk. Martin walked to the door and knocked. On either side of the door Greg had placed a larger rock, each one weighing maybe ten, maybe fifteen pounds.

He heard footsteps and then the door opened. A gust of cold air hit Martin and it felt good on his face and arms. There stood Jenny in cut-off Levi's and a white t-shirt. She had her hair up off her neck. Martin always loved it when Jenny put her hair up. He loved the way her neck looked. Jenny stepped into the doorway with her mouth open, looking at him. Martin stood there, holding the box with the dog in it, and looked back at her. The dog made no noise. Martin thought, for an instant, of the girl in the ice cream store.

"What are you doing here?"

"I brought you something," he said, lifting the box a little higher in the hot air. "I brought you something."

Jenny didn't move. For the moment, there was no sign of Greg. From inside the house came the squeals of young children at play. Martin stood on the doorstep, savoring the cool air pouring out of Greg's house.

"It's too late," she said. "Don't you know it's too late? You were supposed to pick them up at nine o'clock."

Martin held the box in front of him, but Jenny made no move to take it.

"Just go," she said.

"I came for the kids."

"Then I guess you're out of luck."

Jenny stepped back inside and slammed the door. Martin hesitated a second then beat the door with his free hand.

"Open up," he yelled. "I want my kids!"

There wasn't any answer. He felt foolish. He couldn't imagine why Greg didn't come out and tell him to shut up and leave. Martin stood there for a second, then turned and walked back toward his car. The dog was silent. Halfway down the walk Martin bent down and picked up a rock. He aimed at the picture window and threw it as hard as he could. He missed. The rock hit the vinyl siding and bounced off with a dull thud. Still no Greg, and no other sign of Jenny. He thought about throwing another rock, but he decided against it. It was just too hot to do anything.

He turned toward the car. Before Martin could take two steps the front door opened and Greg came running out.

"Hey, did you throw a rock at my house?"

Martin turned around and stood there. He held the pet carrier at his side and he stood there looking at Greg.

"I asked you a question. Did you throw a rock at my house?"

Jenny stood behind Greg, and Martin saw Donna and Jeremy huddled together around Jenny's legs. The four of them stood there staring at him like the perfect angry family.

"I just want my kids. I just want to give my kids a dog." Martin's voice broke, and he felt more ashamed than he had ever felt in his life. "I just wanted to give the kids this dog." He held the pet carrier in front of his chest, so Donna and Jeremy could get a good look. "I just want my kids."

"You'd better get the hell away from my house, Martin. If you know what's good for you, you'd better leave."

Martin felt something stiffen inside. Weren't those his children? Wasn't Jenny his wife, before Greg showed up? Martin took a step toward the house. Then he took another. Greg and Jenny and the kids stood there watching him approach.

"Martin, I said get the hell out of here." Greg's face was red. He pointed his arm at Martin as he spoke. Martin kept walking toward the house. He was going to give this dog to his children and nothing would stop him. He was going to do this and then take the kids away.

Greg took a step forward, and then another, and then he and Martin were inches apart. They both stopped. Greg slapped his hand down and knocked the pet carrier out of Martin's grip. That was it, all Martin could handle. Martin cocked his right and ripped a hook at Greg's jaw. Greg saw the punch coming and leaned out of the way. He grabbed Martin around the waist and threw him onto the well-kept grass. Greg was on top of Martin, his knees pinning Martin's shoulders to the ground.

"I don't want to hurt you," he said. "Not in front of the kids."

"God damn you," Martin said. He wasn't struggling, wasn't making any effort to get Greg off of him or to stand up. Greg held him down for a few more seconds, then, in one motion, he stood and walked back to the door, where Jenny and the children still stood. Greg stood there with his arm around Jenny, looking straight ahead.

Martin stood up. He was shaking, and he felt like he might cry. Jeremy and Donna stood beside their mother, ten feet away. Both of the children were sobbing.

"Daddy," Jeremy wailed. "Daddy Daddy Daddy." The boy broke away from his mother and ran to Martin, both his arms stretched before him. He wrapped his arms tight around Martin's leg, still sobbing. The little girl ran to him and grabbed the other leg, crying loudly.

"My babies," he said, bending down and hugging them together. Martin sat down on the grass, still hugging his children. The three of them sat there, Martin now crying with Donna and Jeremy.

"I brought you a present," he said, reaching for the pet carrier. The children cried more softly now but still held tight to his legs.

"What'd you get us?" Jeremy asked through a sniffle.

"I got you a dog, son." He opened up the box and there laid the puppy on its side, not moving, not breathing.

"Doggie," said Donna. "Mommy we got a doggie!"

"Why's he lying there like that?" asked Jeremy. "Is he dead?"

"The doggie's dead," wailed Donna. "Mommy!"

"Maybe he's not dead, sweetheart," Martin said, but looking at the puppy he was sure it was. Martin looked up at Jenny. She was different. The anger had drained from her face.

"Go," she said. "Take the kids. Go see a movie or something."

"Thank you," he said. Martin stood, one crying child on either side of him. "Wanna go see a movie?" he said. Both children nodded.

"Okay, let's go."

Jenny walked over and took the pet carrier from Martin. For just that moment the four of them were together and Greg was cut off, watching from the porch.

"I'll take care of this," she said. "You go on."

"Come with us?" Martin asked her.

"No, Martin," Jenny said.

"Daddy, I think the dog's dead," piped Jeremy.

"What do you expect, son," said Greg. "Your father's a loser."

This time when Martin lunged at Greg he was fast enough. His haymaker caught Greg high on the left ear and staggered him. Martin hit Greg again before he could recover, and Greg went down. Martin kept hitting Greg in the face until Jenny dove onto his back and dragged him off. Martin backhanded Jenny, and she crumpled.

Martin found one of the stones beside the door and picked it up. It weighed at least ten pounds. He brought it down hard on Greg's face. Greg made an awful noise, but he didn't get up.

The kids stood there wailing. Martin grabbed each of them by the hand and ran to his car. He got them inside and locked the doors just as Jenny ran up and began beating on the windshield. Martin realized she was hideous. He was terrified. How could he have ever loved this woman? He had to go somewhere, anywhere. He had to find someplace where he could get away from all of this. Just this second he had no idea where that place might me.

"Bastard!" Jenny wailed. The children kept up a steady shriek.

Martin started the car and pulled away, knocking Jenny to the ground. He didn't look back.

Ditto

I was sitting on the porch bothering nobody when the little girl walked over and poked me with a stick

"Daddy," she whined, "when do we play Christmas?"

It made my heart hurt to hear her pained little voice, and I downed my Iron City before I turned away so she wouldn't see me crying.

"There'll be no Christmas for us this year, little darlin'. Your mama has left us and taken all my holiday cheer with her."

"But Daddy," she wheedled, "Mama ain't dead. She's just living in sin with Fat Sammy, the discount plumber from the other side of the tracks. Just because Mama's diddling another don't mean we should forsake all Christian tradition."

The girl wiggled her bottom and her golden curls glittered like Jello creams in the silky afternoon sun. Her cut-off jeans and frayed t-shirt twinkled in the westerly breeze.

"But Cupcake," I protested, "don't you know that Christmas is no more than an orgy of capitalistic horror, designed to part honest men like me from their hard-earned dollar?" I tried not to look at her, to avoid the persuasion of her twitch and twitter. "Peaches, did I ever tell you of the time your mother tried to kill her fifth-grade history teacher by stabbing at her again and again with a number two pencil? It was terrifying. The old broad was a bitch, true, but—"

"But nothing, Daddy-o. I want my Santy Claus, and he better come tonight." She sat on my knee and rocked back and forth, humming some Christmas song that I used to know. She was breathing and swelling up with each breath. I needed to go inside. I wanted to use the bathroom, but the toilet had been blocked for a week. If it was any other time, I'd call Fat Sammy, but the thought of what he was doing with my old lady made my heart hurt again.

"Darlin'," I said, squeezing her knee, "let's go in the house and I'll give you some Santy." I couldn't keep from sweating as I crept in the door. The girl followed with that horrible wiggle. I could smell the toilet as I took her by the hand.

"Merry Christmas, Daddy," she said.

"Ditto," I said. Seems like there ought to be another country where you could do something about all this.

A Simple Enquiry

On the morning of July 14 at ten a.m., two plain clothes detectives arrived at Borges's door and directed that he accompany them to the central police station. He was surprised and more than a little frightened, but Borges offered no resistance. He went quietly, even deferentially, to their automobile.

"Police," the big one had said. "You will please come with us."

The big one, the one in the ill-fitting suit, got behind the wheel, while the little one with the face of a weasel got in the back seat with Borges. They rode along for almost five minutes before anyone spoke again.

"What's the matter? Why am I being arrested?" asked Borges.

"Who says you're being arrested?" It was the weasel-faced policeman who spoke. "Did we tell you were being arrested?"

"No, I suppose not."

"Good. Remember that later. Be certain of it." This from the driver.

"But—"

"No buts, Borges. Just be quiet and cooperate. That's all we're after, your cooperation with the authorities."

"Yes," said Borges. "Certainly."

Ten minutes later the big cop in the bad suit pulled the car into the parking lot at police headquarters. The three men got out of the car, and the officers led Borges into the station.

They went through the public waiting area, down a long, brightly lighted corridor and, when the corridor ended, through a black door with a word stenciled on it in white: Interrogation.

The smaller man directed Borges to sit on one side of a small table. There was a lamp on the table, but it was otherwise bare. Borges sat where he was told, and the police officers sat side by side across from him.

"Tell me, Borges, what is it that you do?"

"Do?"

"Don't be stupid. What do you do for a living?"

"I'm a writer. I write books."

"What sort of books do you write, Mr. Borges?"

"Novels, short stories. Works of fiction."

"And why is it you do this, Mr. Borges?"

This question stumped Borges. He wrote because it was the thing he did.

"Could you explain the question?"

"Surely a man who makes his living with words can grasp the meaning of so simple an enquiry. Why do you write these books?"

"Because I am compelled to do so, I suppose."

"Compelled? By whom, Mr. Borges? Who on earth compels you to write books of fiction?"

"Why, no one. No one but myself."

The police officers exchanged a look, and Borges watched their faces, trying to determine the significance of that look and of the questions they asked.

"And if the authorities required you to stop? What then?"

"To stop?"

"Certainly. Are you hearing impaired, Mr. Borges?"

"My hearing is fine."

"Then please answer the question. If the authorities required you to cease writing, would you comply?"

"This is absurd. What possible reason could the authorities have for requiring that I stop writing?"

The small policeman, the one with the face of a weasel, flipped a switch on the base of the lamp and Borges was assaulted with a brilliant glare.

"Do you feel it is your place to question our actions?"

Borges was silent for a moment. He knew the answer that he should give, but he couldn't bring himself to say it.

"Perhaps. Yes, perhaps I do."

"And why is that, Mr. Borges? Where ever did you get such an idea?"

"I don't know. Look, see here, what's this all about? I haven't done anything wrong!"

"Has anyone suggested you've done anything wrong?"

"Well—"

"Of course not. We're just asking questions, just talking like gentlemen. Of course, we already know quite a lot about you, Borges. We know why your wife left you. We know what you ate for dinner Wednesday before last. Maybe we know your dreams even, huh?" The small man allowed himself a smile in the direction of his partner and a quick chuckle that sounded like a rat terrier barking. "You know the mayor, slightly." This was not a question, but the small detective said nothing else. He sat across from Borges and looked him in the eye.

"I don't see how that could matter to you." Borges had met the mayor just twice, both times at public functions and each time only to exchange the most banal pleasantries. The first meeting had been at a forum on public decency which Borges had attended more out of boredom than to learn about, or to promote, public decency. The second was at a fund raiser for the public library. Also, he had voted for the mayor's opponent in the previous election.

"Please don't trouble yourself over what matters to us," said the small man. "Don't give that another thought, but you still have not answered my question, Borges. Will you stop writing if I tell you that you must?"

"No, I don't think I could stop writing. I don't think that I could."

"Certainly you don't mean that. Be very careful of what you say here. Words can haunt a man."

"I understand that very well, sir."

"Good. Now, I will ask you once again. Be very sure in your answer. If we were to require you to cease and desist from your activities as a writer, would you do so?"

"No."

"No?"

"No."

"Very well, Mr. Borges. You have been most helpful to us. You are free to go."

"Thank you," he said, feeling the words in his mouth as if he were licking shit off a boot.

The officers stood in unison, and the small one motioned for Borges to do the same. He pointed toward the door and smiled at Borges.

"You can find your way out? You can get a taxi home?"

"Yes, certainly."

"Good. Goodbye, Mr. Borges."

"Goodbye." Borges started for the door, but before he had taken his second step the small man spoke again.

"Remember your loyalties, Mr. Borges."

"Yes," said Borges. "I will remember my loyalties." He walked slowly out of the room, picking up speed in the corridor until he was practically running as he passed through the waiting area and out onto the sidewalk. The sun was high overhead, and it was already uncomfortably warm.

Borges realized he was sweating and noticed his hands were shaking. He walked away from the police station and found a pay phone a block away. Soon a cab was there which picked him up and deposited him at his house.

For the next three days, Borges waited for something else to happen, but it never did.

There was no midnight knock on his door, no secret envoy sent to whisk him away, nothing at all out of the ordinary. On the fourth day Borges began to calm down, began to believe the whole thing had been a misunderstanding, or perhaps an elaborate joke of some kind. It was absurd, of course, that anyone would play such a joke, but Borges could put no other face on it, could come up with no other explanation.

He sat at his breakfast table that fourth morning, drinking coffee and preparing to read the newspaper. That was his common breakfast, coffee and the paper. Borges took a sip from his cup and looked for the first time at the headlines. The lead story caught his attention such that he almost spit out his coffee. Instead, he swallowed quickly and read on. "MAYOR INDICTED IN SEX CASE," screamed the headline. Borges quickly scanned the story. It was alleged that the mayor had engaged in a most odious sexual affair with a young girl, a twelve-year-old who was related to him by marriage. According to the indictment, his wife had begun to suspect wrongdoing and confronted the mayor. After he denied her accusations, she went to the girl who told everything. The wife then went to the police and the indictment quickly followed. The mayor had been arrested and freed pursuant to a hefty bond.

"Sweet Jesus," said Borges. "Can this be it? What can this have to do with me?" He put the paper on the table, along with his coffee cup, and wandered into his living room. The shades were closed, and he poked a finger in one so it opened slightly and he got a view of the street. He saw nothing unusual.

Whether out of fear or caution or simple lack of inspiration —Borges himself couldn't say which—he hadn't written a word since the day the detectives came and took him to the police station. Now, for the first time in days, he felt inspired. Borges went to his typewriter and began working. He wrote for a solid three hours, and when he stopped, he had completed a draft of a story of a mayor and a young girl and an affair between them. In his story there was nothing of the evil that must have accompanied the actual events. Rather, Borges took another route, attempting to show beauty in the horror, romance within what must otherwise be called rape.

The story was rough, certainly, and greatly in need of polish. But, all in all, Borges was satisfied with his effort.

He had just finished reading over his story when a knock sounded at the door. Borges laid his story beside the typewriter and walked across the room to open the door. Standing there on his porch were the two detectives who had questioned him previously.

"Hello, Borges," said the small one. "Have you seen the paper?"

"Yes, I've seen it."

"Do you mind if we come in?"

Borges thought of his pages, sitting in plain sight beside his typewriter.

"Now isn't convenient," he said.

"We'll only be a moment."

Borges hesitated but felt powerless to resist. What possible excuse could he contrive that would stop them? He knew there was none. He allowed the men inside, but walked quickly toward the kitchen, ushering them along.

"Coffee?" he asked. "Would you both like coffee?"

"Coffee would be fine," said the small man. "Wouldn't coffee be fine, Dietz?"

"Yes," said Dietz. "I could go for some coffee."

The policemen each took a chair beside the table while Borges busied himself pouring coffee for the three of them. He always made a full pot in the morning, so there was plenty left now to go around.

"Too bad about the mayor," said the small man.

"Yes," said Borges. "I saw the headline. Some kind of scandal."

"He was sleeping with a child."

"Dreadful," said Borges.

"Happens every day," said Dietz.

"Every day," echoed the small man. "It happens every day."

"I suppose it might," said Borges. He had poured coffee into three cups and was now carrying them to the table. "Of course, it's none of my business."

"But it was in the paper," said the small detective. "That makes it everyone's business."

"Perhaps. I don't know."

"Borges, I'll get right to it. It may happen that you will be called to testify in this case."

"Testify? Me? You yourself said you knew that I'm barely acquainted with the mayor. What could I possibly say that would have any bearing on this case?"

"You're a writer," said Dietz. "You're a big man. People will listen to what you say."

"And what is it you expect me to say?"

"Only the truth, Mr. Borges. What else?"

"But I don't know the truth. I have no idea what happened."

The small man nodded to Dietz who stood and walked past Borges and into the living room. He returned moments later with the pages Borges had typed that morning.

"Is this the truth, Borges? This that you wrote today?"

Borges felt sick in the pit of his stomach. He felt himself sweating.

"That's nothing. Just speculation. Nothing at all."

"But it's what you do, Mr. Borges. How can it be that the thing a man does, the thing a man is compelled to do, is nothing? I ask you again, is this that you've written today, truth?"

"It's the only truth I know."

"Then you are a sorry man, indeed."

"But you haven't even read it. How can you judge me?"

"We've read what we need to, Mr. Borges. We make judgments as they are necessary.

Will you get dressed please? I'm afraid you must come with us."

Borges, not expecting visitors, was still in his pajamas and bathrobe. Dietz followed him into his bedroom and watched as Borges changed into pants and a shirt, put on socks and shoes. The two of them then walked into the living room where the small man waited.

"Are we going to see lawyers? To talk about the trial?" asked Borges.

"In good time, sir. Come, we must leave now." Each detective took an arm and led Borges to the car. Like before, he rode in back with the small man while the larger one, Dietz, drove to the police station. The three of them got out of the car, and the detectives led Borges into the building. This time they went through a door just off the waiting room, a door Borges hadn't noticed before. They went through the door and down several flights of stairs, finally ending up in a poorly-lighted hallway. The detectives pushed Borges forward, and he stumbled a couple of steps further.

"Stop," said the small man. They stood beside a steel door with a tiny window near the top. The small man produced a key and unlocked the door. "Inside," he said, pointing into the room. "Now."

Borges considered running, but it was apparent there was no place to go. Maybe if he cooperated, everything would be fine. This was all beyond him, anyway. This couldn't be happening the way it seemed to be. He took a deep breath and stepped inside the room. It was dark in there, the only light coming from the dim hallway. The small detective shut the door behind Borges. It was suddenly very dark, indeed.

"What are you doing?" yelled Borges.

"It's for your own good," said Dietz.

"Yes, said the little one. "If the public found out what you have written about the mayor, how you condone his raping that child, my friend, you would be ripped to pieces. You'll be fine.

There's a sink in there for water and complete plumbing facilities. Someone will bring you food."

"Wait! You can't do this! Let me out of here!"

But it was too late. The door was locked, and the detectives had gone. The only reply Borges received was the echo of their footsteps as they walked slowly down the hall. Much later—a day, maybe two; it was impossible to tell—Borges again heard footsteps in the hall. They came quickly and, when they were just outside his door, stopped. He heard the fumbling of keys and prepared himself to bolt as soon as the door was opened. The key turned in the lock. No one had been around with food and Borges was weak with hunger, so when he tried to bolt and ran instead into Dietz, he bounced to the floor. Dietz was not alone. He escorted a man whose head was encased in a burlap bag. Dietz shoved the man inside Borges's cell and locked the door. The faint sound of footsteps quickly faded. Borges, silent, slumped in the corner. He could just make out the other prisoner who lay sprawled on the floor, whimpering. After what seemed a long time, the man removed the bag from his head. Borges took this as an opportunity to speak.

"Who are you, my friend?"

"I'm no one. Please let me be."

Though he had only heard it a few times, Borges recognized the voice at once. The man whimpering on the floor was the mayor.

"So, Mr. Mayor, it has come to this."

"Do you know me?"

"Who doesn't know the mayor?"

The whimpering stopped. In the dim light, Borges saw the other man stand and straighten his bearing.

"And you are?"

"Borges. I'm Borges, the writer."

"What?"

"Yes, Borges. Do you remember that we met?"

"Forget our meeting. You're the one who's ruined me. You're the one who published those filthy lies."

"I did no such thing. I saw a story in the paper, but somebody else did that."

"More lies. It was all a mistake, a misunderstanding. Everything was fixed. It was going to blow over, and then today your story appeared. Front page. It was sordid, awful. They came and got me and put me in here."

Borges started to speak, but before he could get the words out, the mayor sprang across the room and landed on him. Fists flew, both men kicking and biting and scratching, a battle royal, a fight to the finish.

Upstairs, in the office they shared, the two detectives drank coffee and read the morning newspaper.

"That Borges," said Dietz. "What a writer."

"Yes," said the small man. "He has great talent." They sat there in the office, drinking coffee and reading the paper as the morning passed into noon. It was a quiet day so far, just the way they liked it. Dietz put his feet on his desk and the small man didn't even bother to scold him. In the grand picture, such things are of almost no importance.

Epiphany

"Twenty-three poems," he says. "Twenty-three in one night." The sheer number overwhelms him, as though he knows it would be impossible for anyone to write that many poems in one night. Still, he keeps telling people he did it.

"I wrote twenty-three poems last night," he says to his woman. She stares at him and doesn't say a word.

"I wrote twenty-three poems last night," he says to his boss. At quitting time, there's a three-word note waiting for him in the office: "You're finished here."

He picks up his paycheck and leaves, heads toward his house. On the way he passes a church. Inside the church is a janitor who has been working on one poem for fifteen years. It's the only poem he knows, the only one he will ever attempt, and he has never shown it to a soul. He despairs of ever finishing.

The man of twenty-three poems in one night has no way of knowing about the janitor and his one poem. He passes the church as though it weren't there and keeps walking. He has things on his mind.

That night he tells his woman that he lost his job. She cries and accuses him of being lazy, a no good bum.

"You and your twenty-three poems," she says.

The poet understands that she is correct. He closes his eyes and says a prayer to God. "Why hast thou forsaken me?" Across town, an identical cry crawls its way toward the heavens.

A Constant Battle of the Flesh

It was way past dark when Daddy got mad and squealed his truck out of the driveway. He and Mama had been arguing on the telephone, and she finally said something he just couldn't stand, and he slammed the receiver down and stomped out of there. He liked to go down to Ireland's sometimes to drink beer and cool off, so I figured that's where he was heading. I had that day come home for Christmas, and I guess Virgil didn't know I was there. After Daddy left, I stepped outside to get something from my car. That's when I saw Virgil at the back of the trailer, standing on a couple of cinder blocks he'd stacked up back there, right by Eula's window.

Eula's my little sister. She's nineteen years old and a college freshman, and if I do say so, exquisite. Virgil had stacked those blocks up back there and was peeking in the window at her. He lives right next door with his wife, Cheryl, the one who spent five years as a professional wrestler. The whole family always called her fat and stupid, even though she looks more than a little like Mama. You'd think she would have known what was going on and stopped it, but she didn't, and now here he was peeking, and I had to jump in and get involved.

I cursed the f-word under my breath and jumped over the porch rail. Virgil heard me and took off running back to his trailer. He made it onto the porch in two strides and was in the door like smoke. I knew better than to follow him in, but I did it anyway. I don't like hurting people, and I didn't know what I might do when I caught him. Virgil made it into the living room and was fumbling around with his telephone when I grabbed him and dragged him out the front door. We grabbed and clawed and so forth on the porch, and I was starting to feel kind of foolish, like I'd overstepped my boundaries, when Virgil shifted his weight and lost his balance. He had a pretty good grip on me; and, when he fell, I fell. We both went tumbling over the porch rail.

That's when I think he got the brain damage, if he really has anything at all. They're trying to say it happened when I kicked him in the head, but I don't think so. He hit the pavement pretty hard with the back of his skull; and if his brain is screwed, that is surely where it happened. That's nothing compared to what happened to Daddy. He got goodly snookered at the bar, wasted, blind-dog drunk and wrapped his pickup around a coal truck on the way home. It was a miracle before God that he survived at all. He lost both legs at the knee and landed in a coma that lasted three days, though the doctors predicted he might never wake up. He had to stay in the hospital on an extended basis to overcome his dire injuries and get some heavy-duty physical therapy, and that's why I stayed on after Christmas. Eula was alone in the trailer, and me being her only able male relative capable of watching out for her, it was a duty.

But that's a different story than the one I need to tell. This was all a few weeks ago, and for a long time Virgil drooled and played at not being able to speak in complete sentences. He spent a lot of time out of sight, and word around the park had it that he was lying in bed with a fucked-up brain. When he did appear, he walked with a limp, unless he forgot or didn't think anybody was watching. I figured he was planning a lawsuit of some kind. We're cousins on Mama's side, but things like that don't much matter to Virgil. Hell, I forgot about the business with Eula almost as soon as it was over. It's hard to blame a man for gawking at her, the way she dresses in those tight pants and sweaters, the way she flaunts herself in public, not to mention in

41

her own home in front of her very family. I'd be lying if I said I hadn't sneaked a peek at her a time or two when we were growing up, or even more recently.

A few weeks ago she came out of the shower naked without realizing I was home. I caught a good look at her titties, and I can still see them in my mind, full and young and golden. By God, Virgil, such breasts! I can forgive a man needing to see such undeniable beauty, such intense perfection of form and function, the essence and life's blood of the world. Even if it's my sister. That's what Eula looks like and I can't deny it any more than I can deny a lightning bolt, a hurricane, or a shooting star. If she wasn't my very sister I would be gazing into her window, too, no doubt, but it would be wrong, and anyone who cared for her would be duty-bound to kick the living shit out of me.

That's what I needed Virgil to know. We'd been avoiding each other since the fight, but he and the missus still lived next door to Daddy's trailer. So one evening after Andy of Mayberry went off, I walked over and knocked on his door.

"Who's there?" It was Cheryl's voice, the wife.

"It's Laurence. Is Virgil in?"

She clomped to the door and opened it halfway. She had on her robe, bright red and silky like a circus tent, and nothing else underneath, it looked like.

"Virgil's sleeping. What the hell do you want?" From what I could see of her—only the central portion of her body was visible, with large portions on both the left and right disappearing behind the door itself on one side and the door frame on the other—Cheryl had put on some weight. I made a quick scan and guessed she was up to almost three hundred pounds, maybe three-fifty. She was, as they say around here, fat.

The woman had her hair pulled back haphazardly from her face, and her skin took on a red cast the way it always did when she was mad or excited about something. Her breasts strained their thin cover, rising and falling with her breath. A vision flashed into my head of wallowing in that abundant flesh, suckling, suffocating, floating in a sea of bliss and nipples.

"When he wakes up, would you give him a message from me? Would you say that I forgive him?"

Cheryl stared, clearly unsure of what to make of me.

"What?"

"I said, I forgive him."

"For what?"

"For peeking at Eula's boobies." I had known for years that Cheryl was slow, very, but it was still exasperating to try and carry on an intelligent conversation with her. It took a second for my words to sink in, but, when they did, she threw the door open wide, so hard that I swear I heard it crack.

"Peeking at Eula? Why in the fuck would Virgil want to peek at that boney thing when he's got a real woman at home to pleasure any time he wants? Hell, what she's got shouldn't even be called boobies." She pulled open her robe and, naked underneath, were the two largest breasts I had ever seen. They were spherical and full, not sagging like you would expect with such a large woman, and the areolas were pink and round, twice the size of silver dollars. The nipples were full and pointed. "These," she said, "these are boobies!"

Cheryl was shouting, and I was amazed and scared and horny, and I would have probably jumped on her and tried to ride if about that time Virgil hadn't yelled from the bedroom to ask what all the commotion was. I heard him stomp out of his room, and I knew I should run, but I couldn't, not with Cheryl standing there, immense and purely hot, her robe still open and showing me everything she had. One word exploded in my mind: *Beauty.*

"Cheryl, I need some blessed sleep," I heard Virgil say as he turned the corner into the living room. "Would you please shut the fuck up?" He didn't see me at first because Cheryl blocked his view. Cheryl turned ninety degrees and stood in profile between us, her breasts still exposed and pointing. Virgil saw me at the same moment that Cheryl saw him.

43

"You!" he hollered and lunged for me. Cheryl reached out and grabbed my collar remarkably fast for a woman of her bulk and pulled my head into her chest. She still had that wrestler strength, and it looked like I was about to be double teamed. But, instead of holding me for Virgil to pummel, she caught hold of him as he tried to sail into me.

"Just what in the hell are you doing up walking around and talking for anybody to see?" she spat out, shaking Virgil's head, which she had in a sleeper hold in the crook of her arm. "And what the hell were you doing looking at that stick girl's boobies? Ain't I enough?"

"Oh lordy," Virgil said. "Honeybear, that hurts. Loosen up, I tell you!" But Cheryl had us both in tight headlocks and showed no sign of loosening her hold. Virgil and I were nose to nose, and if he was like me, he had a nipple in his ear.

"Told you," he choked out, "didn't look at no boobs. Laurence made that up." That made me mad, so I took a swing and cuffed Virgil on the cheek. Cheryl let out a moan, a yell like a wounded beast, and squeezed both of our heads as hard as she could. I was suffocating and it hurt like hell to be squeezed that hard. Somehow Virgil managed to get his foot up and he kicked me right in the nuts, hard, and then he did it again. That's when Cheryl let us go. He was all over me like stink on a goat, and the next thing I remembered was waking up in the hospital, right next to Daddy.

I was bandaged and in splints and traction, with a plaster cast on each of my arms and a complicated stainless-steel appliance hooked to my head to keep my broken jaw immobilized.

"Well, I'm a mess," I muttered, best I could. It hurt tremendously.

"Damn straight you are. Fucking lunkhead." I recognized Daddy's voice, though I couldn't see him yet. My head was in a fixed position, and he was off to the side. He was in a wheelchair, and he wheeled over and pinched me hard in the ribs. He used to do that to Mama a lot back when she lived with us. I flinched and tried to yell ouch and it hurt my jaw so bad I needed to scream, but couldn't, so I just lay there, tears coming from my eyes, unable to move or speak, clueless.

"Well, you did it, didn't you?"

"Sir?"

"You had to go fight that trash again and get all flummoxed." He pinched me again, a good one, twice as hard as before. I hollered through my clenched jaws and hurt, hurt, hurt.

I was in the hospital for almost a month, and when they finally let me out I had a permanent limp and recurring headaches, and vision that sometimes went blurry when I got excited. Daddy came home, too, and he still fights with Mama on the telephone every chance he gets. Well, good for him. The fortunate thing was that my injuries canceled out Virgil's, so he didn't pursue a lawsuit. I thought about suing him and Cheryl, but decided against it. Hell, they don't have anything but that old trailer and a rusted out Oldsmobile.

Things have gotten back to normal lately, and Virgil and I even buddy around some now. He still slurs his words on occasion, and even limps, so who the hell knows about his brain? But if he's bothered by it, he doesn't let on. Just last week he was down at the trailer drinking beer. I was all laid out on the couch, convalescing, and he was still wearing the neck brace he's had on ever since Cheryl tried to kill us both. Eula was taking care of us, bless her, the way she does. She brought us a new round of Iron City and I couldn't help but notice how thin she looked in her short shorts and halter, almost sickly. I caught Virgil taking a peek at her butt when she bent over, but I didn't care. Hell, you've got to feel sorry for a man like that. My heart is in the trailer right next door. All fleshy and huge, comforting in her strength and terror, I cannot forget or wander. Her name is Cheryl and I adore her. Virgil promises me naked pictures soon, and for only twenty dollars. I swoon in contemplation.

Jeanie Leanie Shoots the Sewers

Orville

The day Jeanie Leanie died I had to take the bus downtown to see the chiropractor because my neck got all twisted and the pain was terrible. Jeanie Leanie and I had been together so long that when I found her floating in the tank I jerked around and let out a holler and that's how I hurt my neck. It hurt me real bad, having to take Jeanie Leanie and flush her down the toilet, but I did it, then ran down to the bus stop and waited.

I had to wait almost twenty minutes, and it was raining. Those bus stops keep out some of the weather, but they don't keep rain from blowing in on you if it really wants to, and that day it did. I sat there with the rain blowing in on me, trying not to think of Jeanie Leanie shooting through the sewers. My neck was so hurt I could barely move my head.

Maxine

We were running a little late because of the rain. That and the fact that there was a wreck on Lucash Street and everybody got held up while the ambulance and police and wrecker got there. Ordinarily I always get to my stops on time, but today some fool had to crash his Buick into the side of the Washington Bridge. He didn't seem too hurt, but it looked like the little girl in the car with him pretty much had her head cut clean off. By the time I got through traffic I was running almost ten minutes behind. As if that's not bad enough, when I got to the Oak Street stop, there sat Orville, stiff as a board, staring straight into a driving rain. It looked like the sky was crying on him.

Dr. Beyer

I never see patients without an appointment. It's just one of my little quirks.

Unnamed Sheriff's Deputy

Man, what a wreck. That guy hit the side of the bridge like he meant to blast through to the other side. We tested him for alcohol and drugs, but he was clean as a baby. All he got was a busted shoulder. That little girl was decapitated. I don't know if it was shock, and I can forgive a man in shock, but he sat there in the car laughing. He was sitting there beside that little headless body, laughing when I pulled up.

Orville

The bus was packed. There was only one seat open, and it was beside a dirty little girl holding a plastic doll in one hand and a radio in the other. She had headphones on, but I could still hear the radio through them; it was that loud. I might have stood, but there was my neck to think about, so I sat down beside her and heard the word of the Lord.

Gracie

Sure, I listen to the preacher shows sometimes. They're a hoot, even if they're probably right about all of us sinners burning someday in the fire and brimstone. "All the more reason to enjoy it while you can," I say. No way was I happy this smelly little man sat down next to me on the bus, but I zoned into the preaching and didn't pay any attention to the creep who smelled like fish.

The Spurned Lover

I gave her everything, but it wasn't enough. Whoever said to get them young and raise them right didn't know what the hell he was talking about. Still, I wanted to check myself out when I hit that bridge, not kill Jessica. I just wanted to do something nice for her birthday, and all she could say was it was over. I can't really say why I was laughing when the cop showed up, but he didn't seem to like it much.

The Deputy Again

I didn't mean to hit him, but he just kept on laughing. I have a teenage daughter myself, and I'd hate to think how I'd feel if that was her lying there dead and some son of a bitch laughing about it. I probably shouldn't have used my flashlight, but once you start something like that it's hard to quit.

Maxine

I watched Orville in the mirror, sitting next to that little tramp with her headphones and devil music. Poor Orville. I love him so.

Orville

"Sinner, be saved," that's what He said. Death comes to every man. He didn't say anything about fish, but I knew that on my own. The bus stop was two blocks from Dr. Beyer's office. When the driver opened the door for me, she gave me a dirty look.

Maxine

And he left, my inamorata.

Midge, the Receptionist

So I told Mr. Snell that the doctor wouldn't see him unless he'd made an appointment at least forty-eight hours before. I hated to do it, because he was soaking wet and his neck was all twisted and sore, but those are the rules. He stood there for a minute, and I thought he was going to beg, but finally he just turned to leave. That's when the doctor walked into the waiting room.

Dr. Beyer

Well, rules are made to be broken, aren't they? A man feels generous on his daughter's sixteenth birthday.

Orville

I was on the table when the police came and told the doctor something. He had my head in his hands and was giving me an adjustment as they walked in the door. I guess they surprised him because he snapped me around harder than ever before. I felt my spine pop clean to my toes. Never felt better in my life. Being next to God can make the whole day go better, even in the face of tragedy. When I left the room, I heard him make an awful noise.

Maxine

Orville was there an hour later, waiting for me. The rain had stopped, and he looked like sunshine, standing on the sidewalk. I opened the door and smiled. "Hello, Orville," I said, and he looked back, and after a moment he smiled.

Orville

I don't know how she knew my name, but it's all part of the mystery. I felt as good as a man has a right. Maybe I'll even get another fish. You can't replace a friend, but sometimes you take a chance. Sometimes it works out.

Maxine

Everybody sit down. No smoking, please. Here comes the road. Easy does it.

The Night Before

She pulls the letter from under the receipts in her desk drawer and shakes out the pictures. He is more than twice as old as the last time she saw him. Impossible. She remembers the sand in his voice and his hands, warm, holding a book of stories by that Argentine writer whose name she never could pronounce. Upstairs, her husband, oblivious, watches television. The kids fight somewhere, and one of them screams. Screaming is something she understands. Maybe tomorrow she will throw these things away. The letter and photos, she means. She is almost sure of that.

She Finds Herself Dancing

In another universe, a hand touches a great machine. There is a button which, when pressed, brings motion and light. With that, the world begins. Again.

***

The visions come when Mary dances. When she's talking to her grandpa or the servants or hatching a plan with her plucky friend, Louise—to keep from being taken to an orphan's home— she's too caught up in the problems of the world. But when she dances! That's when she feels free and alive, and the visions come and, of a sudden, she holds the dim, impossible memory that this has happened many times before. The visions are always the same, only with changing faces.

Always, she sees a dark room, large, and filled with people. They sit in row after ordered row, and it's a little creepy, the way they stare at her, but she likes it, too. It feels like this is what she's made for. She finds it odd that some of them eat handfuls of something they pull from boxes on their laps, and occasionally she gets embarrassed because she notices a couple, usually toward the back of the room, kissing and touching one another in a way that would surely give Grandpa fits, but none of this makes her stop dancing. In fact, she never misses a step, which is funny, because the dances are impromptu and complicated and sometimes done with an unexpected partner: Jubilee, the butler;

plucky Louise; her old grandpa; even Napoleon, the Great Dane that Grandpa loves to curse but secretly feeds scraps from the table when he doesn't think anyone is around. She's considering this as Jubilee demonstrates a mean soft shoe and then points to her, clearly meaning that now it's her turn to do the same moves, or maybe something better, and how in the blue-fucking hell could he expect her to do this, as she's never done the first soft shoe in her life? But, lacking a choice, she surrenders to her body and her steps are flawless. It makes no sense.

And then, there it is, the crowd. She allows herself to consider the word, "audience." There must be two hundred people out there, watching her. She's glad to know she can't possibly fail, but that certainty removes some of the luster from the thrill of the performance.

About twenty-five rows back, a boy and a girl sit close together. His arm drapes her shoulders, and she molds to his body like still water along a smooth lake bank. They aren't like other couples she's seen, so desperate and obvious. She sees them like this and feels a vacancy in her heart.

The boy and girl hold her attention for a while, but inevitably she notices the light. How did she miss it until now? The light is brilliant and, now that she has realized it is there, all encompassing. It is more important than all the faces, more important than the couple she was watching. She realizes she is of the light, sustained by it, but still a separate entity, just as Jubilee is separate and Grandpa and Louise. Everything. But if everything is of the light, then everything must ultimately be the same. Not made of the same thing, or really, really similar, but the same one thing. Damn, that's confusing, but it seems to be the only honest answer. Mary wants to know the oneness of returning to the source.

Maybe this light tells her story again and again. Why wouldn't it? Maybe it brings forth other worlds, just as real as hers, but impossible to visit. If it can illuminate one world, why not an infinite number of worlds that loop through time?

Beginning, living, ending, beginning again. And what if there are other lights? This is all too much. Mary's stomach starts to churn. "Maybe this is what freedom feels like," she muses.

With every step, every smile, she tries to pull herself out of the moment which now she understands to be endlessly repeating. She tries to pull outside of herself and return. Return. She feels dizzy, blissful, and terrified, remorseful at her separation from the source. And then she feels the beginning of separation from the place in which she seems to exist and the tug toward merging with the light. But it is never enough. Once, she believes, she almost made it, found herself for the smallest moment in a blazing, white-hot universe and wondered if this were heaven or hell.

Does Jubilee have these visions? Louise? Napoleon? Anyone? When Jubilee picks her up and throws her toward the ceiling, she spinning in mid-air, he catching her as she falls, is he trying to push her through to this new world? Does he know it is impossible? Is that why his eyes look so sad and full of love above that brilliant smile?

Just as an answer begins forming in her mind, she stomps her left foot onto the floor a good ten inches in front of her right and extends both arms forty-five degrees from her body, palms forward and fingers splayed. The dance is over.

Almost as soon as she is still, the vision is gone. Like each of the countless times before, once the vision leaves, she forgets she has had it. What remains is the vacancy in her heart that she cannot now fathom. If only she could tell someone, Louise maybe, but whom she talks to, what she says, these things follow a path of their own design. After a while, she puts away the ache, hides it until it really seems to be gone. And then, for no good reason, she finds herself dancing.

Running With the Dogs

I don't know where the dogs came from. The car was parked in front of a dry cleaner's shop in a good part of town, and I picked it because it looked like it could move. It was an old Caddy, red, with fins, a boat, but there was something about it that said speed. I hotwired it and drove down Main Street with the radio playing jazz. I had no idea what was in the trunk until I had a flat an hour later, and I stopped to fix it. That's when I found them, eight German shepherds wrapped in garbage bags loaded in the trunk.

It struck me as funny. That wasn't just because I'd been drinking Turkey since noon, either. I could have chosen any car but it's just my luck to pick one filled with dead police dogs. That's what my granddaddy called them, or sometimes German police. He always kept one while I was growing up. The one he had longest was Nato, named for the North Atlantic Treaty Organization. I guess he figured they were both designed to protect him from the kind of people who go around doing awful things like stealing cars.

Anyway, I didn't know what to do with these dead dogs. My first reaction was to get sick. I mean, there was a smell. You didn't get it much until you punched open a bag, but then there it was, big as anything. I held my breath as I pulled the tire and jack out from under them and changed the tire.

I wanted to get the dogs out of the car, but I didn't want to touch them, so I left them back there and made up my mind to find another car the first chance I got.

One good thing about the dogs was that they got my mind off of Linda. Ever since she left, I've been going bat shit, and I like to think that's part of the reason I stole that car to begin with. It's not like I do that sort of thing all the time. My friends and I boosted a few cars when we were in high school, just went for rides then left the cars off in town good as new and never ever got caught. We'd get us some beer and drive around the back roads like we were immortal and bulletproof, but—other than the time Jimmy Parchette scraped the quarter panel of old man Bullard's Buick on the side of a tree—we never so much as scratched any of them. Jimmy worked at his father's garage and the funny thing was old Bullard brought it in there to get repaired, and Jimmy was the one who did the job. I don't know whether he gave Bullard a break on the price, but I remember that Jimmy did a damned fine job on that car. When he was done, you couldn't even tell where it had been damaged.

I guess we were kind of wild back then, but I hadn't done that sort of thing for a long time.

The thing about Linda was I saw it coming but didn't do anything about it. I could see she was restless. I was working all the time at the lumber yard, and it's the kind of work where you come home tired at the end of the day. She'd want to go out and eat, or go get a beer or maybe see a movie, and I'd tell her another time, baby, because I'm so tired I just can't make it.

I give her credit, she hung in there for a long time. We'd been married five years, almost to the day, when she pulled up stakes. I guess she saw that anniversary coming at her and decided to get out of the way before it hit her right in the face.

She left me a note, took her clothes and the VW Beetle her daddy gave her when she was in college, and that was it. The note read, and I quote, "I can't take it any longer, Billy. I'm gone and I won't be back. Sincerely, Linda." Sincerely. If that's not a fucked up way to end a goodbye note, I don't know what would be.

After that, I started drinking and didn't stop except for work. It wasn't a month before coming in hung over so much—and still drunk more than a few times—got me fired. Buster Barnes said he hated to let me go, that he liked me and all that, but he believed I was becoming a danger on the job. "Sober up," he said, "and come talk to me again." Then he asked me about Linda, and I told him to mind his own fucking business, and I got the hell out of there.

Unemployment insurance kept me going for months. I didn't want a job, and I didn't look. I just cashed my check every month and paid my bills and spent the rest on groceries and cigarettes and drinking.

So maybe I wasn't completely responsible for stealing this car. I mean, living the way I was had really messed up my mind. At first I was just going to find a car and go for a ride, just feel myself moving down the road, just the way I used to feel it when I was a kid. I figured I'd go down the back roads like we used to, maybe drive around all night, then park the son of a bitch somewhere and nobody would really be worse off because of it. Then I got to thinking that there really wasn't much reason to drive around in circles and then just stop. I figured, "Why not just drive?"

But the dogs scared me. What kind of person goes around with a trunk full of dead dogs? Maybe the car belonged to a vet, and he was doing something with the carcasses. Maybe they had rabies or some shit, and maybe I already got it on me when I busted open that bag and looked at one of them. Maybe the car belonged to a psycho who went around murdering German shepherds and collecting their skins or mounting their heads in his rumpus room. A man like that would probably not be someone you'd want to mess with, even if he ended up being a squirrely little nothing. Guys like that can pull a trigger, same as the next man.

Like I say, the smell was bad. I knew I had to get away from this nightmare, but I didn't feel right just abandoning the dogs. For whatever reason they had come under my care, and something inside me wouldn't let me leave them to be maggot bait in that hot trunk. So I bought a shovel at the Wal-Mart in Lorraine, and I drove way out into the country to bury them.

There's this pond where I used to fish, and I figured that was as good a place as any. It was full dark by the time I got there and a beautiful, clear night with a three-quarter moon and the sky lit up with stars. I pulled off the road just up from the water and found a level spot and began digging a hole.

I had never once brought Linda to this place, even though it was one of my favorite spots on earth. I thought about that as I dug. I thought about a lot of things, and they all were things about Linda: the way she cooked me bacon on Sunday mornings and got it crisp and didn't let it curl up like a lot of people do, the time she got mad and threw a whole set of dishes at me, and the way she looks when she's asleep, curled up like a baby.

It took a couple of hours to dig the hole. I wanted to make sure it was deep enough to cover all of the dogs and keep other animals from digging them up, so I put my back into it and dug a good five-by-five grave.

Then there was nothing to do but get them out of the trunk and into the ground. I went for the first one and picked him up, being careful not to touch anything but the garbage bag he was in. The dog was heavier than I expected. I had heard about dead weight, but I never really understood the term until that point.

I took the dog over to the grave and dropped him in, and he landed with a dull thud. I noticed right then that everything was quiet. The frogs were quiet, the crickets. There was no sound other than my own breath. The silence was huge. I stood there and looked first into the hole where the dog lay in his garbage bag, invisible inside the shadow of night and then I looked up at the sky and all the stars shining down on the dead dogs and me.

It hit me then, how funny this situation was. I was an unemployed drunk, abandoned by my wife and in possession of a stolen car and the bodies of eight dead dogs which stank to high heaven and which I was now in the process of burying in one of my favorite, almost secret places, a place I never even shared with my wife. The laughter started in my belly and worked its way to my mouth, and I stood there laughing for two or three minutes before I was able to stop and get the rest of the dogs into the hole. It was maybe another hour before I got them all in there and covered up good.

I rolled down all the windows and drove back toward the highway. There was no reason in the world for me to go home. I figured I'd drive through the night and maybe dump the car in Little Rock and hop on a bus, maybe head out to New Mexico or over to Tulsa to see if Linda's parents knew where to find her. As it turns out, I didn't go to either of those places, or at least I haven't yet. The first bus out was bound for New Orleans. I'd never been there before and had always wanted to see that place. I left the car at the terminal and bought me a ticket for the Big Easy. I headed south, and I've been there ever since. I keep thinking I should be running away but then I figure why bother. There's a secret world out there that nobody knows about, where dead dogs come with stolen cars, and the strangest things are sometimes buried in the most wonderful places. These are two things I know. Maybe someday I'll find Linda, and the two of us can figure what this all means, but right now I'm staying put. Getting better, I think. Sometimes I really believe it.

Swarm

It was sometime before dawn when Mama looked over at me and whispered, "God damn it, Gerald, those bastards are here and they're here now. Now's the time to swarm! Are you ready?" She said this under her breath, her voice still lovely beneath the rasp she'd developed in the weeks we'd been hiding in the abandoned farmhouse, that part of her still alive, still the woman I had known for all that time.

She wasn't my mama, you understand. That's what we all called her, all of us who found ourselves hiding out there in the hills, the ones of us who found our way to that old house, a refuge, a place to catch our breath until the night before when Cadman saw the smoke down in the valley, and we all knew it was only a matter of time before a patrol combed the hills and found us.

Still, where was there to go? We'd all been about everywhere and found not one single place worth staying, no place where the soldiers weren't in command, no place we weren't eventually run out of. I guess we were all tired of running. The farmhouse was nice, nothing palatial, but enough for us, even after so many of us showed up there, so many of us on our last legs, last dreams, gathering there by chance for one last go at life, for what now appeared to be our one last stand.

We were lucky as hell that Mama found her way there, too. I knew her from the old days at the hospital, back when I was a doctor and she was a nurse. Even though she was at least fifteen years older than me, back then I used to order her around. Sarah, check this man's temperature. Sarah, see to that one's medication. She did it, too, but that was the old days. I can't imagine what she'd say if I tried a stunt like that now, though I suspect it would involve my getting my teeth handed to me via her clenched fist. In an odd sort of way, I found that exciting.

We'd been sleeping in shifts as a matter of course, but since Cadman saw the smoke, none of us had really dropped off at all. My nerves were alive with the day and the danger, and even more so as I heard the soldiers tromping up the hill. I guess we all heard them about the same time, because there was a general silence in the living room, the room we were all gathered inside, faces looking to faces in mute fear and anger and expectation, until Mama whispered to me her call to battle.

The thing was, I was her favorite. It was clear to me and surely to everyone else that this was true, and I suspect there was more than a little jealousy over this in our new family. None of it got to me, though I'd be lying if I said it didn't please me that she liked me best, but it was only right, as far back as we went. We had a history, and it's not like I was unkind to her back at the hospital. Not even close. I only ordered her around; I didn't beat her. It was the job.

"God damn it," she said.

The troops were obviously getting close now. Their footsteps crunched heavily upon the rocks and undergrowth and it was even possible to get a hint of conversation every now and again.

"Swarm!" Mama said, louder this time, for everyone to hear. There was a general nodding of heads and murmuring of assent. It was true, we'd all had enough. Here we were, backed into nothingness, and it was swarm or be swarmed. Mama raised her hand and the room went quiet, everyone listening to the approaching patrol. I felt my hands tighten around my Louisville Slugger, the only weapon I had, and even at that a better one than most of the others. Some had sticks and a couple of the women had frying pans. Cadman had a bucket of rocks. Mama herself had nothing more than a hatchet, a small hand axe she'd found out back when she first got there. Of course, she was the first to find the farm, and she picked up the wickedest looking weapon she saw and made it her own.

Just by luck, I was the next one to show up, and she damn near took my head off with that hatchet before she realized who I was. She got me a good whack, a gash deep into my left shoulder. Damn thing took weeks to heal, and I might have died from it if Mama hadn't been a nurse. She stitched me up, watched over me. That was a close call, but I didn't blame her for anything. These days, it's hard sometimes to tell just who is the enemy and who's not.

While I convalesced, Mama kept things running. She went out into the woods and scavenged food. Mostly it was roots and nuts, berries, that sort of thing, but sometimes she brought in game and cooked it on the old wood stove in the kitchen. She was a dead shot with that hatchet. I used to listen to her practicing, throwing it against a middling spruce. She bragged to me that she could cleave a rabbit at twenty paces, and I believed her.

Once I was able to get up and around, I found the bat stuck away in a closet and claimed it for myself. You could pretty much tell what order folks arrived by the quality of their weaponry. Poor old Luther, the last one to find us, all he had was a pillow case, but he had it crammed full of rocks and dirt and animal droppings, whatever he could find in the yard. Luther wasn't as bright as the next fellow and that's a fact, but as long as the seams held, he had a bag that could knock a man's head off.

Mama spoke again.

"Are we ready?"

"Yes!"

"This is our moment!"

"Yes!"

"Let's get those bastards, then!"

"Yes! Yes! Yes!"

We rose as one body, Mama before us but all as one. She strode to the door and flung it wide. The soldiers weren't quite to our clearing but were clearly only seconds away. She turned and faced us all. Standing there like that, she was the most beautiful thing I had ever seen. She must have been sixty, and her body was full, fleshy but not fat. She was heroic, magnificent. I wanted, more than anything in the world, to fuck her into unconsciousness.

I looked around the room and saw Cadman. He was watching Mama too, and close, maybe closer even than I was. It gave me a pain to see his eyes on her like that; and if my mouth hadn't been dry, I would have spit. It wasn't just that his eyes were on her. Hell, everybody's eyes were locked forward, studying her every move. It was something more with Cadman, something easy to recognize if you knew it yourself, and it hurt me just to think about it. Love's that way.

"Swarm!" she hissed.

I nodded with all my heart and so did Cadman; and though I didn't see the rest, I am certain everyone did the same. Cadman looked my way, and our eyes locked, just for a moment. I sneered at him, and he sneered back. Mama walked outside and we followed, me second in line, then Cadman and the others. We hadn't talked about what plan of attack we might follow, too scared or dumb I guess to look that far ahead, but the entirety of our futures seemed to be held hope and hostage in that word Mama kept repeating, that word, swarm.

And by God, that's what we did.

The patrol emerged into our clearing unready—I soon understood—to encounter anyone. They tromped around like bulls, looking this way and that, but mostly down at their feet, looking to make sure where they stepped in the dense undergrowth. This was a mixed gender patrol, a ragged bunch to be sure, out in the field for who knows how long, rounding up stragglers like us, taking them back to the camps or sometimes, rumor had it, killing them on the spot.

We swarmed. Or maybe we pounced, the way we jumped straight at them. But whatever name you want to put to it, we were smashing. Mama led the way, screaming as she ran. It was an awful scream, and I think that's what did it for us. I think it scared the troops half to death, but it got my blood high. My pecker was hard as oak, and my balls clanged like steel bearings. Mama ran straight for them, hatchet raised high above her head and took out two boys before they knew what hit them. It was her nurse's training, of course, that told her where to strike, and she used that training well, bringing her hatchet down hard and economically on the first two soldiers, before the rest of us caught up with her and began whaling away.

In the first seconds the troops, frightened and disorganized as they were, got off a couple of shots, but without taking much time to aim. Bullets whizzed this way and that, but we were resolute and fierce and we jumped on them with a vengeance.

It was over fast. Mama got a girl, and I took out the three soldiers nearest me with my Slugger. I tried hard not to notice which sex I hit. Later, in the aftermath, I saw one of them was female. Cadman hit several soldiers with rocks and the others had great success with their sticks. Unfortunately, Cadman got in the way of one of my swings and I took him down, a hard fast swat to the head with great follow through. Luther got in one good swipe with the pillow case before it broke apart and sent rocks and dirt and shit flying over the battle, but with that swipe he got a man square in the face and put him down forever. Soldiers littered the ground like spent wishes, blood splattered and, save one, dead, turned at odd angles beneath the sunlight, even then gathering its courage toward a hot, beautiful day.

I sat on the ground and wept. I'd taken an oath when they made me a doctor, and it said nothing about cracking the skulls of youngsters with a bat, even if they were trying to do me harm. But it was more than that, more than a simple betrayal of a professional credo. I wept because I liked it, because it felt good to sink hard, lacquered wood into those people, and because I

64

knew it should not. And I wept for Cadman, whom I could have easily missed with my bat if only I had wanted to.

Our side suffered no casualties, except for Cadman, and Luther who had taken a slug in the leg, right after he split his pillowcase on that unfortunate soldier's head. He lay on his side, baying at the blue, blue sky. I went to him and checked his wound and found it, thank God, superficial. The bullet had passed through his leg so all there was to do was fix a bandage and wait. Neither antibiotics nor pain killers were within our reach.

Cadman was beyond the help of anyone but God. He was in a better place, as my real mother used to say when somebody crossed over to oblivion. I choked up when I looked at him, lying there in his broken skull and blood, but I remembered the eyes he had for Mama and bore his death like a man.

The one member of the patrol still alive lay on her side, holding her belly and moaning. Through her dirty, snarled face I could see she was young and pretty. Even though they'd been sending women out on patrol for years now, it still shocked me when I saw one up close. I bent over her and tried to look at her injury.

"Ow!"

"Sorry. Just trying to see where you're hurt."

"Where's it look like? Jesus."

She held her belly like she might hold a child in her arms. There was blood on her hands and on her uniform. It made me tingle to see it. I never was much in emergencies. Even back in the old days I stayed out of the ER as much as possible.

"Listen, I'm a doctor. You're hurt, and I'm going to help you."

"Like you helped the rest of them?"

"That was different. It's over now. Do you want my help or not?"

She gave up. I guess the pain was too much or maybe she was scared of bleeding to death, but she moved her hands and let me look at her belly. She had a broad gash just above her navel, but it was longer than it was deep. My guess was that Mama had tried to gut her but didn't get in a good enough swipe. Ordinarily, in hospital conditions, her injury wouldn't have been much of a deal, but what she needed was stitching and I had no way to do that. What suture we had at the farmhouse had been used on my shoulder when Mama whacked me.

"I saw you hit that man with your bat," she hissed through gritted teeth.

"This was a battle."

"No, asshole. I saw you hit that man on your side. I saw you break his head, and I think you did it on purpose."

"Why, I never!"

"Like hell. You smacked him right in the temple with that piece of lumber, followed through like you were batting cleanup for the Dodgers. Ouch!"

"Sorry. Look, you need stitches and I don't have any way to do it here. If I let you go, are you going to bring another batch of soldiers here to wipe us out?"

"Probably." She looked me in the eye, and I knew as soon as she reached camp she'd have them right after us. But she was so young. So lovely.

"Well, I'll just have to risk it. I'm still enough of a doctor and a man not to let a young woman bleed to death if I can help it. Now that the battle's done if you can stand, do it, and get going."

She managed to sit up, then used her hands to push herself to her knees and swayed to her feet. She stood unsteadily, no more than a foot in front of me. Her face was beautifully freckled, her swimming blue eyes just a bit too close together and her hair was the color of corn. She leaned forward and kissed my cheek. It was the first time I'd felt like a human being in months. A kiss like that from a young girl, even on the cheek, was enough to make me forget about wanting the old woman with the hatchet.

"Thank you." She was still crying, but it was just tears, no sobbing or catch in the throat. She held her belly tight with both her arms.

"I'm a doctor," I said, wishing she would kiss me again. I thought about it for a second, then bent forward and gave her a peck on the forehead.

"Doc, you better get your ass out of here before we come back."

As she spoke, I noticed Mama out of the corner of my eye, just a glance at first, then I did a quick double-take and saw she was staring at the girl and me. Her face was pure hate.

"Run!" I screamed. The girl turned and headed for the trees. She might have made it had her stomach not been cut, but that slowed her down. Mama let fly with her hatchet and caught her in the back of the head, the blade stuck three inches into her skull. The girl went down and didn't get back up. I was afraid, for a moment, to look at either of them. Finally I turned my eyes toward Mama, because of the two, I knew she was the only one capable of hurting me. She glared at me for a second, then spit.

"Swarm!" said Mama, standing over the corpse of another soldier, a young man of maybe nineteen, maybe less, somebody young enough to be her grandchild, or perhaps my son. Luther was still yelling and if she heard his cries, she made no betrayal of it. Mama stood there with her gray hair loose and tangled, her eyes flashing fire.

My first impulse was to go to the girl and see if I could help her, but I already knew she was beyond that. What I had to do instead was help myself.

There was something in Mama's eyes, something beyond survival, a hatred so pure that I shivered just to be near it, a hatred that wouldn't understand mercy, or weeping for the dead on either side of the fight. And beyond that, love.

I looked at the other faces around me, faces burning with hate and vengeance. It was a beautiful moment, but it made me weak in the belly, and I couldn't help thinking of the future, gripping my bat tight, holding it against the next blood it might be called to spill. Cadman. Cadman, I thought, what have I done?

"Swarm!" I screamed, holding my Louisville Slugger high above my head. It was the most terrifying moment of my life and the whole blessed bunch of them cheered.

Bulk Rate

Jack hates being a mailman. He's hated it for years, but it's the job he has, and he's scared of looking for another, so he soldiers on. What he hates most is all the junk mail he has to carry. Bills, personal letters, packages—okay. These things people bring upon themselves. Many times they even enjoy receiving them. But junk mail, all those envelopes: "YOU MAY ALREADY BE A WINNER! URGENT MESSAGE, OPEN IMMEDIATELY! A SPECIAL OFFER FOR FOLKS OVER FIFTY!" All that useless crap.

The sheer weight of this mail is staggering. Jack figures that over the years he's carried more than seven tons of junk mail for more than a hundred miles. His feet ache just at the notion.

He starts reading stories in the paper about disgruntled postal workers. There was a guy in Omaha who went crazy and shot up the post office. Another fellow in Maine did the same thing. It seems like every time he turns around another postal worker has blown his co-workers away.

The thing he can't figure about it is why the newspaper stories always refer to these guys as "disgruntled." What kind of word is that, anyway? Jack thinks of a number of words that might describe the way he feels: dismayed, disorderly, dissatisfied, distended, upset, pissed off, enraged, perplexed, mad, angry, insane, sore, queasy, sad, loopy, irregular. But disgruntled? Too tame. Too tame especially for those guys already over the edge, the ones who brought their guns to work.

He starts hoarding the bulk rate material. He's supposed to deliver everything assigned to his route. To do otherwise is a felony. Jack doesn't care. He starts keeping it and stashing it in his house. Maybe if it doesn't get to the potential customers, the advertisers will see their investment is losing them money and will cut it out. Maybe Jack will single-handedly bring down the junk mail industry. The savings in trees alone would be staggering.

Soon his living room is filled with flyers from Food Town and K-Mart. "BIG SALE THIS WEEK! UNBELIEVABLE VALUES!" Next to them sit the Publisher's Clearinghouse envelopes. Big, thick, hideous bundles of waste. They make a huge pile right next to Jack's rubber tree plant.

A couple of weeks of this and Jack is running out of room. He's got a small place anyway, and the junk mail just keeps on coming. His kitchen fills up, his bedroom, his bath. One day his supervisor calls him into the office. Says there's a problem. Says it seems like some of the mail isn't being delivered.

"Frankly, we're concerned. We can't help wondering where all this mail is going."

Jack doesn't respond at first. He sits there looking at his supervisor. Both are aware that he—Jack—looks like hell. What with the Kroger circulars in his tub, he hasn't been able to shower in five days.

"We want to help you, Jack. We want to make sure the mail gets through."

"DON'T MISS BIG BARGAIN DAYS!" says Jack. His supervisor looks nervous. Sweat forms on his face. There is a button on his desk and he pushes it. "YOUR IMMEDIATE ATTENTION IS REQUESTED!" says Jack. "DATED MATERIAL, OPEN AT ONCE!"

The office door opens and two big men in postal uniforms enter. They look to the supervisor for instructions.

We've got one, boys," he says. "Careful, now."

The bigger of the men leaps on Jack and wrestles him to the floor.

"NOBODY BEATS OUR PRICES!" says Jack. "WE WILL NOT BE UNDERSOLD!"

The big man holds Jack down while the smaller one applies the restraints, the gag, hood, and irons. Together they drag him out of the supervisor's office, down the hall and to the room that is kept for just this purpose.

The supervisor has a pretty good idea where the mail has gotten to. He calls and arranges for someone to check out Jack's place and retrieve anything, um, unusual, they find. He looks at a pile of applications gathering dust on his desk. It's hard to get a job with the post office. Good hours, good pay. Benefits. He's going to make someone very happy.

The supervisor picks up the first application from the pile and starts dialing a phone number. He's thinking to himself, absolutely without irony, *SATISFACTION GUARANTEED!*

An Ugly Monkey

I was drunk when I came out of St. Mark's, but that seemed okay because I was drunk when I went in. I'd thought about going to confession, but when I saw the booths and Jesus on the cross and the Holy Virgin, I couldn't bring myself to do it. It was dark in there, hot and humid to suffocation, and I was sweating hard. The sad little crucifix I'd bought last week was just a lump in my pocket. Hell, I'm not even Catholic, not since I was a kid, so what good could any of this possibly do? Margaret wasn't taking my calls, and I had my doubts about anyone else listening either. It seemed the best idea was just to go on home.

Outside it was cooler. I was walking down 34th Street, minding my own business. From the shadows between Tony's Lounge and The Szechwan Palace slid this greasy little fellow in a white polyester suit, and he hissed at me. You know, "Pssst, pssssst," like in a movie. I kept on going because I had enough troubles of my own, and I figured this probably meant more. But then he said it, and I stopped. I had to.

"Hey meester, wanna buy a menkey?"

He said it just like that, just like Peter Lorre. At first I couldn't figure out what he meant.

"A menkey?"

"Yes, a very fine menkey. See?" He made kissing sounds with his lips and from behind him somewhere scampered this big, ugly monkey. God yes it was ugly, probably the ugliest monkey I've ever seen. Maybe the ugliest monkey that ever was. Its fur was gone in big patches and its exposed skin blotched white and red. There were open sores here and there on its chest, and one of its eyes was brown and, so help me God, the other was blue. Just as blue as the sky. It wore lurid-green Bermuda shorts with orange stripes down the sides. The thing stood about three feet tall and clamped between its teeth was a cigar, smoked about half-way down. Quick as shit, it climbed up the guy's leg and then had its arm around his neck, and he was holding it like a kid. The monkey took a puff from its cigar and blew smoke rings into the air.

"It's magic, sir. Four wishes, four—"

"Get away from me with that damned monkey," I said.

"But sir —"

"I mean now." I turned back the way I was heading and moved on out of there. I didn't even look back, but after a block, I stopped at the crosswalk and felt something grab my leg. I looked down, and there it stood, ugly and smoking, and I swear it smiled at me.

"Get the hell away from me," I hollered and kicked at it. It dodged under my foot and rolled between my legs. Then it hit me square in the balls, and hard. I went double and fell to my knees. I thought for a minute I was going to puke, but I held on. The thing paced back and forth beside me, making those monkey sounds like in the Tarzan movies. Then it stopped and scampered up the side of my body and put its arm around me and kissed me right on top of my head.

Okay, it was just a dumb animal, and it was lost, and its instincts made it protect itself—and now maybe it was sorry. I didn't exactly forgive it, but I was willing to not try kicking it again. I figured White Polyester would be right after us, running down the street, looking for this thing, but he still hadn't shown by the time I was able to stand, so I walked back to the alley where I'd seen him. The monkey followed right behind me. When we got to the alley, the guy wasn't there.

"Eeep," said the monkey. "Eeep eeep eeep."

I tried everything to get the monkey not to follow me. I yelled at it. I cussed it. I almost kicked it, but I figured that wasn't such a good idea. So what could I do? Hell, when a man's lonely and going crazy with it, he sometimes forgets his better judgment. Or maybe he just gives in easy. I went on home, and the monkey went with me.

It was a third floor walk-up, and the monkey kept right with me as I slogged up the stairs. When we finally made it to my room, I opened the door, and it ran inside. I got my emergency pint from the shelf over the sink and poured a glass of whiskey. I needed it. There were big, yellow bananas in the cabinet, from when Margaret was over the other night, the last time I'd seen her, and I figured I might give the critter one after I had my drink. They weren't doing me any good. I just couldn't see eating them after what happened. And of course, there was the crucifix. She'd left that behind, too, and maybe that's why I wandered into the church. I'd been carrying the crucifix in my pocket for days, and every now and then I brought it out and held it to my face and took a deep breath. I did this now and shoved it back into my jacket. I was ready for that drink.

But the monkey had other plans which didn't include either crucifix or bananas. Before I could even get the glass to my lips, it grabbed the bottle from the table. It took a drink and then another, and before I knew it the bottle was empty. Great. Just what I needed, a big drunken monkey with a skin disease. With the booze gone, the thing got mad. It started waving the empty bottle and screaming.

I downed my sorry little glass, and the monkey glared at me. It made a noise from the back of its throat and showed me its teeth. They were big all right—long, sharp and yellow. It made the noise again and closed its eyes then opened them wide. Its eyes sparkled. The brown eye had the look of a dark, polished marble. It was so brown that it was almost black, almost dark enough to be empty, like the mouth of a cave or the gateway to hell. The blue one was sunshine summer skies and ocean waves and, in spite of the monkey's overall hideousness, I felt drawn to it. I might have walked over and petted this thing, but it still looked mad enough to kill. Then I looked close and it was as if the blue eye was becoming huge, baseball-like or cantaloupe. It swelled, became the entire room, and I fell into it, and it wasn't that monkey crouched in the corner but Margaret, big titties and all. It had been more than a week, and I felt myself getting hard. It was Margaret and Mary and a crucifix held between her thighs, winking and my balls sang "Go! Go!" and I went. I was on the floor fumbling my belt with one hand and fondling giant breasts with the other—I even got my fingers into the warm wet goo of cunt—when Margaret or Mary leaned close and bit me hard on the leg. The pain was magnificent. At once it was no longer a woman, but the monkey, and I jumped back and scurried crab-like across the floor.

My God my God I've fucked the thing, I thought. No, not fucked it, not quite, but so close, close enough to feel it hot and slick, close enough to smell. I stood and straightened my clothes and moved my erection so that it didn't catch in my underwear. I couldn't bring myself to look straight at the monkey.

And then it farted. God, what a fart. It was loud and long and rotten. The gas from that creature's belly smelled of hell and disease and everything sick. It was like a cloud from a death house, putrid bodies and shit so bad even the flies wouldn't bite. The very stench of it slapped at me, and I staggered into the wall. I held my breath, made it to the window, flung it open and hung my head out. I gagged and tried to hold on, but up came the whiskey. I watched as it splattered on the sidewalk. Shit, I thought. Shit. I must have hung out that window for five minutes, shaking, until finally the smell began to let up.

When I turned back to the room, the monkey was on my couch, innocent and serene. Its legs dangled toward the floor and its arms stretched out almost the length of the sofa. I watched as it opened its fly and jammed a hairy finger up its ass. What now?

The monkey brought the finger up to its nose and took a deep breath. It shook its head and cried out and waved the bottle again.

"Oh Jesus," I said.

Was I going insane? I didn't know what to do with the damned thing. I didn't have any more liquor, so I called up my pal, Frank. I didn't tell him what was going on, but I asked if he'd bring some whiskey over right away. He was there in twenty minutes, and he brought his girlfriend, Stella. Even though he was going a little bald, Frank was a ladies' man and always had a woman in tow. Lately it was Stella. She was a looker and wore the clothes to prove it.

"Lord God Almighty," said Frank as he walked into the apartment. "Who shit?"

Before I could answer, Stella saw the monkey and the monkey saw Stella. This woman was one of those freaks of nature who get an overabundance in one area but shortchanged in others. While she curved to big and small perfection in all the right places, with the legs, tits and ass of a 1940s movie queen and the face of a two-hundred-dollar whore, Stella was also the only person I've ever known without a sense of smell. She couldn't smell a damn thing. Ordinarily, this would seem to be a handicap, but with monkey fart residue hanging oily on the air, it now worked to her advantage. She was also nearsighted and much too vain for glasses, so I guess she couldn't tell at first what the thing on the couch was. I'll be damned if I knew, either.

"Oh, a doggie. Nice doggie," said Stella.

The monkey sprang across the room and ran its hands up her short red dress and groped her panties. Stella screamed and jumped up and down, bouncing and jiggling and hitting the thing on the head with her purse.

"Oh, Frankie! Frankie, get it off!" She was almost hysterical, and who could blame her? Frank was right there and he did what anybody would do. He tried to kick the monkey away. The little bastard was preoccupied with Stella, so he didn't react quite in time. He tried to duck, but Frank's kick got him pretty square in the ribs. Frank had played some ball in school and it was just like a Saturday back on the field, one more punt for the team. The monkey rolled under the table with a big squawk, then tumbled back toward Frank and, from the floor, planted him a solid kick right in the nuts. Frank went to his knees, and I guess the monkey saw the whiskey he was carrying, because he grabbed the bottle and shot across the room. Frank fell over and lay there moaning. Stella climbed up on a chair, screaming and jumping up and down, holding the hem of her dress tight around her lovely thighs. With each jump her breasts rose and fell in heart stopping rhythm, and her dress rode a little higher on her legs. You might fault the little monster's manners, but you couldn't question his taste. The monkey stood in the far corner. He'd opened the bottle, and now he was drinking in perfect contentment. I sat down on the couch and tried not to stare at Stella. I didn't say a word.

After a while, Frank was able to sit up.

"Jesus Christ, Gordon, what the hell is that that thing?"

"What the hell do you think it is, genius? It's a God damned monkey." Stella and Frank stared at the monkey, and the monkey stared back.

"Eeep!" it said. "Eeep! Eeep!"

"I think it's a chimp," said Stella.

Frank gave Stella a dirty look.

"Well, what the fuck are you doing with a monkey? Anyway, it doesn't matter. I'm gonna kill that little son of a bitch." Frank got slowly to his feet and picked up an ashtray and made as if to move toward the monkey. The monkey put the bottle on the floor, still holding it by the neck, and gazed at Frank.

"I don't think I'd do that if I were you, Frank. He's pretty quick."

I told them the whole story of how I came to have the monkey in my apartment, stopping short of it changing into Margaret or—and?—The Holy Virgin, and the rest of that business.

"Four wishes?" said Frank. "Whoever heard of four wishes? It's always three."

"Don't be a moron," I said. "There aren't any wishes and there's no such thing as a magic monkey."

Frank gave me a dirty look.

"I'm just saying the old guy got the story wrong, okay?"

"Whatever."

"He is kinda cute, though, ain't he?" said Stella.

"Stella, that is without a doubt the ugliest monkey that has ever lived. I think it's got the mange."

"Look who's talking, baldy," she said.

Frank ran his hand across his thinning hair and shut up. It was plain that Stella had hurt his feelings, and I didn't see any call for that. Loyalty, that's what counts. She knew Frank was touchy about his scalp, so she went right for it. Loyalty is a rare bird.

"Come here, little guy. Come to Stella." She waggled a finger at the beast. It was pretty loaded by now, and it did well to stagger over to her.

"Bobo," she said. "I think we should call it Bobo."

"Eeeep eeeep," said the monkey. It sat down beside Stella and patted her foot.

"Good Bobo," she said. "Nice Bobo."

Bobo rested his head on Stella's foot and gazed up. It looked like he had a pretty good view up her skirt, but Stella didn't seem to notice. It didn't matter, however, because in a few seconds he was out cold, passed-out, stinko drunk. Frank retrieved the bottle.

"Hey," said Stella, "It looks like he's got something in his pocket."

I almost said he probably had something in his pants, all right, when Stella reached down and pulled a card from the awful green of Bobo's shorts.

"Listen to this: 'My name is Emil. Please do not give me cigars or whiskey.'" There was another name on the card: The Great Silvera. Stella shook her head and looked at me accusingly.

"You shouldn't let Bobo drink," she hissed. She reached down and stroked his fur. "The poor thing must be old. Look at how his hair's falling out."

Frank had been sulking on the couch ever since Stella's crack about his hair, but now he piped up again.

"Hey Gordo," he said. "You got any more of those bananas left?"

I nodded and caught Stella blushing.

"Hey, honey," said Frank. "Go in the kitchen and get the monkey some bananas. I bet he'll wake up hungry." When she was gone, Frank leaned over to me and winked.

"How'd Margaret like the bananas?"

Frank managed a porno store, and I guess he saw all kinds of things in the magazines and videos he sold. He was the one who suggested Margaret would go for the fruit. All women love that kind of stuff, he said. The crucifix had been my idea, after Frank's, but I didn't see any reason to bring that up.

"She's gone, Frank. I don't think she liked them much."

Frank sat back and nodded knowingly.

"Another frigid bitch," he said. "No offense, Gord." Then he ground his right fist into his left palm.

"So this Silvera guy must be the one who dumped the monkey on you. Let's go find him and kick his ass. Nobody whacks me in the balls and—"

"Frank," I said, "it wasn't Silvera who whacked you. If you want revenge, your boy's right over there."

Frank considered this for a moment and then glared at Bobo, or Emil, or whoever this monkey was.

"Don't even think about it, Frank." It was Stella, back with the bananas. There were seven left from a bunch of eight. "At least if you're planning on going around with me anymore." You could tell Stella meant it, but I'll be damned if I knew why she had such affection for this creature that a couple of minutes earlier had been a second away from raping the bejesus out of her.

79

"You know, Stella, sometimes I wish you weren't such a good lay. Then I wouldn't be so willing to put up with your shit," grumbled Frank.

Stella grabbed a banana and peeled it fast and bit off the top half. It was a ferocious bite and she chewed hard and swallowed. There was a mean look in her eye.

"And I wish you'd quit thinking about all those other women and just concentrate on me! You think I don't know about those whores you run around with? I do! I do!"

As I said, Frank was quite a ladies' man, and I guess it was hard for him to stick with just one woman.

About that time the monkey woke up. First he fluttered up the brown eye, and then the blue one just shot open.

"Eeep! Eeep! Eeep!" The monkey looked first at Frank and then at Stella. He shook all over and did a somersault.

"Well," I said, "what I wish is that this damned thing would just disappear." Frank and I toasted to that, and Stella gave us both the evil eye.

"Hey," she said. "Where's Bobo?"

Sure enough, the monkey was gone. I'd left the window open and the wind was blowing the curtain into the room. We all went and looked out the window. We were on the third floor, but there was a drain pipe that he could have grabbed onto and shinnied down. Anyhow, there was definitely no monkey.

Fortunately, he left the bottle behind. We drank it off and tried to figure the whole thing out, all except the business of my unfortunate hallucination. I still kept that to myself. We even tried calling The Great Silvera, but couldn't find a listing. By the time the whiskey was gone, we were all laughing about it, and even getting hit in the balls seemed funny to Frank and me. Frank and Stella made up and were hanging all over each other, and it was no surprise that when the whiskey was gone, they left too. After that I didn't see Frank or Stella for a while.

In the days that followed, I found myself going by the Catholic church every now and again. There was something about the place that attracted me, but I can't say just what. I was never able to go to confession, even though I was pretty sure I should. I couldn't even pray. The crucifix was always in my pocket even though when I brought it to my face, it now smelled only of wood. After a while, I stopped visiting the church or lingering by the alley between Tony's and the Chinese place on my way home. It was a couple of weeks later that I ran into Frank at a bar. He looked awful.

"It's Stella," he said. "She used to be so great in bed. She had moves like you wouldn't believe. And now, and now...." His voice trailed off. I was about to suggest he dump her and find some new talent, but it was obvious from the pain in his face that there wasn't another girl in the world. For some reason I felt guilty, but not much. We sat and drank and didn't talk.

Frank left a half-hour before closing. It was Friday night and I decided to give Margaret one more try. I walked to the back of the bar where the pay phone was. Before I dialed I mumbled a wish out loud. It was the best I could do. It rang ten times. I let it go a couple more for luck. No answer. Then I thought about Stella. I thought about her jumping up and down. I thought about that jiggle and those amazing thighs. I remembered Margaret and Mary and that crucifix and my balls sang. Even hideous Bobo flashing back into memory and biting couldn't cool me off. There was no way Frank had made it to Stella's place yet. She answered on the third ring. She sounded glad to hear from me and said she'd slip out before Frank made it home and meet me at my apartment. What the hell. Bad pussy's better than none at all, especially if it's human. I hung up and got one for the road. Maybe she'd like the Polish sausage I'd been saving for Sunday dinner. Dead Jesus on the cross in the warm wet dark.

Whoever heard of four wishes, indeed?

Faulkner and Pete

I sometimes like to go and lie down on Faulkner's grave. He has a flat stone, and you can lie there and look up into the day and become lost. You'd think, as famous as he is, there'd always be somebody around there, some mourner or literary type paying homage, but in all the times I've visited the cemetery, I never saw another soul around. It is my own place and Faulkner's, and I go there and listen to the wind whispering through the stones and hope for—what?—some message from the beyond to keep me from fucking up bad, the way I usually do.

The first time I went there was after I was supposed to kill the dogs. My brother, Pete, and I got hired by this fellow out in the county to round up a pack of strays that were killing his chickens. We were supposed to take them out somewhere and shoot them, but when we got them all loaded up in the truck, the seven we were able to catch, they weren't chicken killers to us, just big old mutts with the same hope for life that any of us has. None of them even tried to bite us; and once we had them gentled, they only wanted petting, and if we had brought any food with us, they would have been happy for that, too. I hoped at first that Pete would have more resolve than me, but I was thankful when he didn't. We horsed around with them for a while and then we drove them out to another part of the county and set them free. When we let them go, they sniffed around the car and whined, wagged their tails. We left them like that, just off the road, hoping they could make some kind of life, maybe even get picked up by some good people.

We told the man, his name was Dan Pruitt, that we'd done the job, just like he'd asked. He paid us twenty dollars and thanked us and sent us off. A week later he was on the phone, madder than a snake, screaming that the dogs hadn't been shot at all and that they were back at his chickens. I tried to lie, but Pruitt recognized the ring leader, a big collie-shepherd mix with a black throat. He said he wanted his twenty dollars back and that he'd kill the dogs himself. I told him if he thought he was big enough, he could come and get his money, but he just hung up.

Pete was always a softie, anyway. There was no way in hell we ever would have killed those dogs. Pete liked the collie-shepherd especially and had even thought about taking him home. There was something about that one, though, that Pete saw.

"This old boy needs his freedom," he said.

I guess maybe we should have, but we didn't even feel bad about it when we used that twenty for a night at Ireland's, shooting pool and drinking pitchers.

"Here's to them dogs," Pete said.

"Amen." I was pretty sure at least some of them were dead by then, and my "amen" was as much a prayer as it was agreement with the toast. We nursed it since we were low on cash, but that was a good night. I beat my brother five straight games of eight ball, the last one on the break, and he finally gave up. It was sweet. We never played for money, but the loser had to walk to the bar to buy the next round, not a bad deal that night since Gina was back there, and she was an eyeful.

Of course, neither Pete nor I were ever very fluent with the ladies. I'm inward by nature, and Pete, with his speech defect, had a hard time saying much of anything. I always understood him because we grew up together, and I won't mock him here, trying to imitate the way he talked. His voice was clear to me, and I heard his words plain and fine. A cleft palate was what he had, and a harelip. Born with it. The only time it didn't seem to get in his way was when we were alone together. It's easy to be alone with your brother in a crowded bar or in church.

Daddy always took us to the Baptist services, old regular Baptist, and church was loud with "amens" and "praise the Lords" and singing. That's where we knew Dan Pruitt from. He was a deacon and sat in the amen corner, right up front. Every now and again he'd stand up and preach spontaneously, cutting down the wicked and exalting the grace that was our only salvation. He spoke in tongues sometimes, and it used to impress the hell out of me when I was younger. Eventually, listening close, I heard he was always saying the same sounds, like it was something he'd memorized and that didn't seem quite what the spirit of God would do if he'd invested somebody with light.

It was different with my brother. Inside that church, Pete didn't mind letting fly with the spirit of the Lord, either, getting vocal with testimony and even song. It was a different world inside that church, and it was like Pete was a different person. I never was much for church myself, just went to please Daddy, but sitting there on a hot Sunday morning, unrepentant among the saved, I was often charmed by my brother, a lamb of God.

I don't want to overstate my case, though. Pete could raise hell with the best of sinners, and that never changed. During the week he was feisty and happy to drink a pint of whisky at the slightest provocation, to play cards, shoot pool. I even saw him get into a fight once in Ireland's after this redneck accused him of cheating at pool. Pete took one good lick and then laid in on that ol' boy. After he'd hit the guy three or four times, I had to pull him off, afraid Pete might kill him.

Pete's the one who got me thinking about Faulkner because he used to read his books. I never read any of them myself, but Pete seemed to like them real well. There was one he especially liked called *The Sound and the Fury*. Sometimes when we were down at the bar, he'd see a pretty young thing and say to me, "There's Caddy. There's Caddy Compson," like I'd know what he meant. I guess I did, more or less, if Caddy Compson was a hot little girl with blonde hair and nice tits. He told me she was a character in that book and she would break my heart if I ever read it. One time when he was asleep, I tried to read it, but I couldn't get past the first page. I never told Pete about that.

But Pete loved reading and was proud to be from the same place as Faulkner. I, myself, was sick of old Bill by the time I was out of high school, the way all the teachers tried to cram his books down our throats, and then Pete started reading him. It pissed me off for a while, and then I got used to it. I even envied Pete a little because he had something beyond himself that he could appreciate and love.

On the night we went down to the bar with Dan Pruitt's twenty, the intended blood money, we only got a little drunk. It was enough to get me thinking, though, and on the way home I said to Pete that we should go back out by Pruitt's place and round up the dogs again, those that might still be alive, and take them off some place where they would stay and not wander back for chicken and wind up getting shot. Pete was all for it.

The farm was way out on old Highway 7. We drove out there; and when we got close, we pulled off the road and turned off the headlights and made our way out into the fields. Pete had a small flashlight in the glove box, but we didn't use it for fear of Pruitt looking out his window and seeing us poking around out there. We were really trying to do him a favor, as well as the dogs, but we knew he might not see it that way, us sneaking around his place in the middle of the night. All we took with us were a few lines of rope, in case we got lucky and found some dogs.

It was a beautiful, clear night. The moon hadn't come up yet, but stars salted the sky, and the moon gave off enough light that we could see each other easily. We each had a couple of ropes and we split up, calling the dogs, whistling low, hoping for some small miracle of chance that any of them were still alive.

I went closer to the farm, closer to the hen house where the dogs had rampaged. Pete headed down toward the little creek that ran along the farm's northern boundary. Of course I had no luck.

If the dogs were still alive, none of them here hitting the coop that night. After a while I started getting a little nervous and even felt kind of silly out there in another man's field, chasing after stray dogs that I was just going to set free thirty miles down the road. I decided it was time to give up.

That's when I heard Pete holler, then another voice cussing. I started running, fast as I could, through the field. The night became small around me, and I ran toward where it sounded like my brother had been when he yelled. The field was monstrous, an obstacle course of chunk holes and cow piles and tall grass and weeds. I felt my heart thumping fast, and even the stars were gone from my vision by the time I made it to the creek.

I finally thought to yell Pete's name. He didn't answer, but the other voice yelled an obscenity, and then again, and I ran toward that voice. I saw it all and knew before he said anything else. Pete was on the ground. His left foot was caught in an animal trap, a big one with heavy steel teeth. The scream I'd heard was from him when he stepped in it. Old Pruitt had been hiding out by the creek, drinking whisky, and trying to shoot him some dogs. He'd set the traps for the same purpose, and when Pete got caught and yelled, Pruitt sprang out and cold cocked him with the butt of his shotgun. He hit Pete hard across the face, hard enough to cave in his cheek.

Pruitt stood over Pete with the gun still hanging from his hands.

"God damned trespasser," he said. Then he heard me and looked up and for the first time he seemed to know who we were. I was about to jump on him and, I guess, kill him. He was almost too drunk to stand, but he raised his gun and fired it. He was off, but some of the buckshot hit me low in the gut. I would have probably died, but his wife heard the shot; and when Pruitt didn't come in after a while, she called the law. They found us out there, the three of us, Pete dead and me dying and Pruitt sitting drunk and crying against a tree.

Pruitt claimed I hit him before he shot me, and I got six months for trespass and assault. It might have been a lot more, but the judge took what happened to Pete into consideration, and the fact I'd been shot. Fair enough, I guess, but the worst part was I was laid up in the hospital when they buried Pete. I sure hate that I missed his funeral.

They buried Pete in the same cemetery where Faulkner's buried, but I seldom spend much time at my brother's grave. I visit him and leave flowers, but it doesn't feel right. I know Pete's not there. It's different with Faulkner. There's a plaque a few yards away, by the road, and old Bill is as close as I need him to be, with me understanding that he's not quite real, but almost as real as how Pete used to talk about him. I don't know what else to say about any of this, except Pruitt caught most of those dogs, but he never did get that collie-shepherd that was the leader. That's a hell of a dog, and I pray he's still out there, turned wild, ravenous, tearing through this small bit of country, alive.

Out for Cigarettes

Maggie needs cigarettes.

I was out before to buy some things: furniture polish, Cokes, broccoli, fish for dinner, but she forgot to tell me about the cigarettes, so here I am again in the parking lot at the Bi-Lo, and the place is packed. It's December first and cold, and like a fool, I'm wearing shorts and a t-shirt.

The Christmas lights are going up and twinkling, and it's a cold night, and I'm not happy. But here I am, doing one of my little jobs, when a car pulls up beside me and stops. It's an old car, some old American machine, beat up, nothing you'd ever really notice. The driver's a man about my age, maybe a bit older, a big guy, but there's something about him, some terrible aspect of defeat, sitting in the darkness and the cold.

"Excuse me, sir," he says. Then he tells me his story: hungry, no gas, miles from home, and he is sad and sad and sad, and he apologizes for what he has to ask: The horror of begging.

And I have nothing, just some change, two quarters, two dimes, some pennies, not even a dollar bill. I give it all, of course, and as my hand touches his, I feel it rough and hard and callused, a hand that knows work.

He nods and, I swear, this big man is almost crying.

I don't know what else to do, so I walk away, walk into the Bi-Lo where everyone has money and there is more food than a man could eat in a year. There are men and women, families. There is even laughter, maybe grace, but none of it is real. I buy Maggie's cigarettes with our credit card—we always use the credit card—and in my pocket I find a dime. It's not much, but a little more I could have done. The man is long gone now and, even if he was not, how could I go to him with a dime? What could I say?

Everything is impossible, but Maggie waits for me at home where there is light and food and heat and love, and it is easy to forget the lost dogs, the lost men hungry and miles from home in old American cars you would never really notice, to forget the cold and the darkness, the twinkling, awful, lights of Christmas, two packs of cigarettes and a small coin heavy in my pocket.

Wigs

Finally, the party ended and everyone left. Melissa was in the bathroom when Billy and the last stragglers walked out. I was pulling the tops off a couple of beers when I heard a toilet flush. A couple of seconds later Melissa wandered into the kitchen. I gave her a large smile and handed her a beer. She took it and went back the way she had come. I took a large swallow from my bottle and followed her into the living room.

"Everybody went home," I said.

"Umm." Melissa glanced here and there, her eyes stopping for a second on this wall or that floor or the small oval mirror by the door, or the ceramic knickknack cow or the couch or the plush green chair in the corner; her eyes not on me but everywhere else in the room.

"Let's look around," I suggested.

Melissa nodded and muttered something that sounded like "okay," and followed me through the house. It wasn't long before we found the bedroom and there we were, standing right beside the queen-size bed that was ours for the night.

"I'm getting a little sleepy," she said.

"Yeah," I said. "Me too. Maybe we should lie down."

"You want the couch or the bed?"

I studied her face, hoping for an ironic grin, some sign of a little joke between us, something which said, "Hey, I'm kidding, come here and lie down with me," but there was nothing.

"I thought we could both sleep here."

"Dennis. . ."

"Oh, come on, let's just go to sleep. It'll be okay."

"Nothing's going to happen."

"Right, nothing. Sleep."

"Just as long as you understand."

I went back through the house turning off the lights. When I got back to the bedroom I set my beer down on the nightstand, turned off the lamp, and leaned against the bed to take off my shoes. Light from a street lamp poured in through the window, giving the room a tired glow.

I climbed into bed. Melissa had her back to me. I leaned over and kissed her neck.

"What do you think you're doing? I told you nothing was going to happen!" Everything about her was fierce and final.

I did the single worst thing, the least manly thing I could do. I began to cry.

If I could have just said it then, maybe things would have worked out differently, but I couldn't make my mouth work that way. I couldn't tell her. It had been blocked inside me for too long, and just at this moment it seemed like everything inside me was stuck, everything but tears and hiccups and wracking, awful, sobs.

She calmed down almost at once. I felt her hands on my head, softly rubbing and petting me. I was a strange, overwrought child, and she was a mother trying to make things better.

"Shhh," she cooed "Be quiet. Everything's fine."

I let her gentle me and finally my tears ended and I lay there in the stillness, just breathing, with her hands still rubbing my head.

"I'm sorry," I blurted out. "I didn't mean..." My voice trailed off to nothing.

"Be still," she said. Melissa rolled onto her side, her back once again to me. She allowed my arm to drape over her body and I pulled myself close to her. She didn't move away, though it was clear past all intention that we would do nothing but sleep. I let my hand fall to her breast and still she didn't move.

"You can leave it there," she whispered. "Just go to sleep."

I left my hand on her breast and, miraculous, I slept till the early morning. It was dark outside when I awoke, and the room was still and lovely. I was spooned against Melissa's back, pressed tightly against her like an actual lover. I reached my arm across her body and took her breast in my hand. Her hand shot up to mine and grabbed it and flung it away. Neither of us spoke. After a minute or so, I rolled away onto my other side and tried to sleep again until full daylight.

Eventually, morning arrived. It seemed like we both woke up at the same time, sitting up in bed, scratching ourselves and yawning. I thought of apologizing, but Melissa seemed to have forgotten all about it. She was smiling, playful.

"How's your head?"

"I never felt better," I lied. "You?"

"I feel like I want to go play," she said. "Let's go see what Birmingham's all about."

"I have a feeling it's a hell of a town. Let's go see if I'm right."

We took turns in the shower—no suggestion of sharing—dressed and decided that what we needed was a plate of greasy bacon and eggs and a lot, a whole big lot, of hot, black coffee. Neither of us knew Birmingham, but we drove until we found a Waffle House and ate like we were starving.

After breakfast, we drove aimlessly around the city, then Melissa parked the car in an old section of downtown on an empty street. The buildings were sad and gray. It was a cold, overcast morning, and a wind was starting up. Melissa got out of the car.

"Stay right here" She opened the trunk and rummaged around for a minute then got back inside.

"First we smoke this," she said, holding up the hash and the little pipe. She smiled, merry as an elf, and filled the pipe with hash, lit it and took a deep hit. She held the smoke in her lungs and passed the pipe to me. I took a hit, held the smoke and passed it back to her. We each took two more hits and then she put it away under the seat. I felt nothing. The wind blew a handful of leaves into the air just in front of the windshield, and it looked like a dance. There was poetry in all of this, somehow, and I watched until the leaves blew into the street and scattered. I looked at Melissa, and she looked back. We got out of the car and, not knowing where to go, headed down the block to see what we could find.

Even as far south as we were it was still a cold morning. The cold wind felt good on my face and then I was shivering.

"Are you cold?" I asked her. Melissa laughed and nodded her head fast, two or three times.

"Yes!" She took off at a trot and then sped to a full run.

I caught up with her in front of a store with a big yellow sign painted in red letters displayed above the entrance: "Julia's Wigs."

"We're going in here," she said. Before I could answer, she was in the door and examining the merchandise. There was a dour, sullen woman in the back behind a counter, tending to the cash register, but she didn't say so much as "Welcome to the store" when we walked in, and we ignored her right back. A quick glance around showed we were in a small room with wigs everywhere. Wigs lined the walls and lay on tables running the length of the floor. Big wigs, tiny wigs, slutty wigs, classy wigs, red, blonde, brown, black, and platinum wigs, wigs that almost seemed real, and wigs that looked like they had been designed by the insane. Any kind of wig you wanted, it looked like Julia had it.

Melissa picked up a curly brown wig, put it on, and looked at her face in a mirror. I wouldn't have recognized her like this if we passed on the street. She started laughing and spun around to show herself off.

"Come here," she called to me, "try this on!" Melissa held a long red thing with bangs. It was garish and beautiful.

This was the kind of thing lovers did, or at least it seemed like it should be. Crazy lovers maybe, but weren't they the best kind? I let her put the wig on my head, and she was as happy as a child. I looked in the mirror and didn't recognize the face looking back. Just some asshole in a wig.

We raced the aisles picking wigs almost at random and trying them on, sometimes looking at ourselves in the mirrors, sometimes showing off for one another and laughing, always laughing. It wasn't just the hash. If you had asked me then I would have said it wasn't the hash at all, that I didn't feel a thing. I could have died right then, and it would have been beautiful.

Unfortunately, Julia's Wigs didn't see things that way. The sullen clerk didn't stay at her counter in the back very long once she saw what we were doing. We had worked our way down one side of the store and were starting for the front again on the other when she walked over.

"Hey," she said, louder than you might expect. "Are you two planning on buying anything?" She stood five feet away, glaring. Melissa had on a smart, short, black hairpiece with a saucy curl in the bangs, very sophisticated. I sported something closer to the Dolly Parton look, a full, thick platinum-blonde wig in loose curls that fell past my shoulders.

"Umm" I said.

Melissa shook her head and kept laughing the way she had been since the spree began. "No!" she told the woman in utter glee.

"Then get out of here," the clerk said. "Get out right now." I took off my wig and handed it to the woman, smiling like a baboon. Melissa stood there a moment then, without warning, turned and fled. She was still wearing the black wig, and even as fucked up as I actually was, I understood that she had just committed a crime. I also knew that I was an accessory. The clerk screamed after Melissa, "Stop, damn it! I'll get you!" and ran out the door after her.

I was right behind the screaming woman. She limped on her right leg and couldn't move too fast. I caught up with her at an alley just past the wig shop and, keeping an eye on Melissa's rapidly shrinking form a block further down, shoved the screaming clerk as hard as I could into the alley. I watched her fall a good eight or ten feet away from the sidewalk. I sped to a sprint just as Melissa turned right a block in front of me. I had to get around that corner before the woman made it back to the street, or she'd have some idea of where to send the police in search of us. I ran faster and faster and didn't dare look back. When I turned the corner there was Melissa, sitting on a cement stoop in front of a liquor store. She wasn't laughing any more but her breathing came hard and fast. She still had the black wig on her head.

I grabbed her elbow and kept trotting up the street. She came along easily, and we were soon running fast again. Melissa pointed to a red and white Budweiser sign hanging over the entrance to a bar, and we stepped inside. What the hell, it was as safe as anywhere.

"Two beers," I said to the man behind the counter. He brought them over and we drank them fast. We took the next round a little slower, and by the third we were relaxed and breathing normally, and the danger of arrest didn't seem quite so real.

There was a dartboard there, and we got some darts from the bartender. Melissa beat me three straight games and wouldn't play anymore after that. We drank our beers and listened to country music on the jukebox.

"Come on," I said. "Dance with me."

"No, I don't dance. I never dance."

I asked again, and again she refused. Memories of the night before, my clumsy advances, her breast beneath my hand, my tears and my stupid humiliation rose up like a physical illness in my chest. When she excused herself to the bathroom, I didn't expect her to come back. She did, but it didn't much matter.

95

"Let's go," she said. It took a few minutes to find the car, then we were inside, driving south. She kept the wig on. I wondered who she was. I wondered who I was. Sad, sad, sad. Love is the meanest con I know.

Horseshoes in the Rain

Paul had never beaten Monroe in horseshoes though they had played at least two or three times a week all summer. The horseshoe pits were in Paul's yard, and Monroe would come over and they'd drink beer and toss shoes. Paul's wife, Betty, played sometimes, but usually it was just the guys, and Monroe always won.

On this particular Saturday they weren't playing because it was raining. They sat inside Paul's house and drank beer and listened to the rain. Betty was visiting her mother.

"Fuck this," Paul said. "I'm going to kick your ass, and I'm going to do it right now. Let's toss some shoes."

"Did you happen to notice the rain?"

"Don't be a pussy."

Paul was already up and heading for the door. The rain was coming down hard and lightning split the sky at least once every couple of minutes. "I'm going to toss some shoes," he said. "You do whatever you want." He walked outside and was at once soaked to the skin. Paul took his time walking to the pit, then he picked up the silver horseshoes and threw one down to the opposite post. It was a ringer. He threw up his arms and spun around.

"Did you hear that?" he yelled. "Better come out here. That is, if you have any balls." He threw the other shoe and missed wide to the left. "And bring the beer."

Monroe grabbed the remains of the case and went out the door. "You're an incredible asshole," he said.

"Fuck yes, I am"

Paul walked to the far pit and got his horseshoes. Betty had been gone since before noon. They'd fought about money the night before, and things had been tense until she left. Betty wanted to spend all their extra cash on antiques and toys for the cat. Paul liked to have a little change in his pocket to go down to Spanky's and drink a few. He liked to go down there and shoot pool and drink a few beers with Monroe and the other guys, flirt with the college girls.

Betty didn't drink anymore, and she didn't see why Paul had to, either. She quit after that business with the baby. Four years into their marriage, after they'd given up hope, Betty became pregnant. Paul was tickled and hoping for a boy. He got his wish, but the baby came out malformed, his head a size too big and minus a right leg. They named him Arthur, after Paul's father, and he lived twenty-one days. That was about a year ago and Betty still had all the weight she'd gained during the pregnancy and some more she'd picked up since. Two things she wouldn't talk about, not even with Paul, were Arthur and her weight.

The last time she drank anything was when she was seven months pregnant. It was vodka and she got goaded into flashing her breasts, enlarged and tender, in front of Monroe and his girlfriend, Lou Ann. Paul was there, too, but he didn't say anything. He just got real quiet and drank more vodka. For a while after that he acted funny whenever Betty and Monroe were together anywhere.

"Hand me a beer, man." Monroe pulled one out and gave it to Paul. The rain was blinding. It was almost impossible to see the opposite post. Even through their shirts it felt like they were being pummeled. Monroe got himself a beer and popped the top.

"If there's gonna be any ass kicking here today, I'd better start warming up my boot. Come on, let's lag for break." They always said they were going to lag for break. It sounded cool, like they understood things other people didn't. Monroe tossed one of his gold horseshoes and hit three feet away from the post. Paul's was closer by almost a foot.

"Ha!" he said. Paul reared back his head and let loose with a howl.

"Go for it," said Monroe.

What with the rain and all, they agreed to only play to eleven. After five tosses, up and back, Monroe led by a point, two to one. He was sighting for a throw when out of the corner of his eye he saw something move in the field beside Paul's house. He stopped and peered into the rain and saw it was a woman and she was running toward them. Before she got there, he could see it was Gracie, the younger sister of Betty's best friend. Gracie tended bar four nights a week at Spanky's and sometimes she came over to Paul and Betty's house to visit, usually with her sister. Gracie had on white shorts and a white cotton shirt and she was soaked.

"Are you guys crazy?" she said.

"Yes," said Paul. "Have a beer." He grabbed a can and handed it to her, then he held both of his arms toward the sky and spun around on his heels.

"Where's Betty?" Gracie asked.

"Visiting her mother. Hey, man, are you going to throw or what?"

"Hold your water." Monroe sighted up and threw. It was his second shoe, and like the first, it missed by a mile.

"Don't you know how dangerous this is? What about lightning?" Gracie's hair was plastered to her head, and her bra was clearly visible though her shirt. The pink tone of her skin showed through where the fabric held to her body.

"We don't care about lightning," said Paul. He held both of his horseshoes above his head and shook them. "I've never beaten this son of a bitch, but I will today."

Monroe sloshed over to the beer and got a fresh one. He was thinking that Gracie was a fox. Both she and her sister were foxes. One night a few months back Monroe was walking home drunk and knocked on the sister's door. The sister's name was Stephanie. She lived right next door to a fast food restaurant that specialized in roast beef sandwiches, and he had bought six of them. He tried to coax her into an evening of fast food and romance. She sent him off, telling him she was a vegetarian.

"When do you think Betty will be back?" asked Gracie.

"Don't know. Maybe never."

"Yeah, right." She took a drink of beer.

Paul tossed his shoes and made a ringer and a leaner. "Praise Jesus," he said. He was up six to two.

"Yippee!" said Gracie. Lightning flashed and seconds later came a huge thunderclap. Gracie jumped and smacked her hands together.

"Nice toss," said Monroe. He took a big drink from his can. "This stuff tastes like water," he said.

"Drink faster." Paul finished off his beer in one drink and crushed the can. Then he threw it at Monroe.

"Watch it," said Monroe. He finished off what was left in his can and took his turn. He landed each shot close enough for a point. Paul threw his first shoe and got another ringer, negating Monroe's two points. His second throw missed, but the score was nine to two.

"Yippee," said Gracie.

"Hey," said Monroe. No fair taking sides."

"You make a ringer, and I'll yell just as loud," she said.

Paul threw again and was wide to the left with both shoes. Monroe got a leaner on his second shoe.

"All right!" said Gracie. She bounced a little.

"Sorry I couldn't get you a ringer," said Monroe.

"You did the very best you could," said Paul. They threw the next round, and Paul scored a leaner. The game ended with Paul winning eleven to four.

"Ha!" said Paul.

"Ha, yourself," Monroe said.

Gracie walked over and hugged Paul. She pulled him tight and held him like that for a second, until he pulled back.

"Congratulations," she said, frowning. Paul took two steps back and bowed from the waist, then he took her hand and kissed it.

"No consolation prize?" Monroe said.

"Sorry, I only hug winners."

Monroe thought about saying he'd won the last twenty matches, but he kept his trap shut. After that squeeze, he wondered if Paul wanted him to leave so he could be alone with Gracie. He wondered if Paul had already been alone with her. Paul was always flirting with Gracie when she was behind the bar at Spanky's, and Gracie was always smiling and giggling. Hell, they could've been going at it like rabbits for months, for all he knew. If they hadn't, now looked like a good time to start. Betty could come home at any time, so it would be risky, but probably worth it.

Monroe had thought a lot about Betty since the time she flashed him and Lou Ann. That had truly pissed Lou Ann off. Lou Ann had little titties anyway, and with Betty even bigger than normal, it was plain that Lou Ann was jealous for a couple of reasons. Betty was fat, but looked like she might be good for a tumble. That might be worth the risk, too. Monroe figured she probably wanted it, or else why would she show her boobs?

They were still standing in the rain, and it didn't look like it was about to let up. Monroe decided he'd have one more beer and watch Gracie in her wet clothes. If Paul wanted him to leave, he'd let him know. Besides, Paul was being an asshole.

"Want to go inside?" said Paul.

"No! This is crazy, said Gracie.

"Crazy," said Monroe. He opened another beer and took a drink. Gracie grabbed the gold horseshoes and held them above her head.

"Don't do that," said Paul.

"Want to play?" she shot back.

"Hey, look at the time," Monroe said under his breath. Then louder, "I've got to be going." He stood and swallowed the dregs from his can. Before he could finish his goodbyes, Betty's red '82 Grenada turned into the driveway. Betty got out of the car, all smiles. The rain slicked her clothes against her body and made her look even fatter than usual. Monroe took a good look and nodded his head.

"What in the world?" she said.

"I just kicked Monroe's ass," said Paul.

"I hope it didn't hurt too bad," Betty said. "You don't look much worse for the wear."

Monroe smiled.

"Hi Betty," said Gracie. "I came over to talk to you and these guys made me watch them, of all things, play horseshoes."

"Well, honey, let's you and me go inside and dry off. These idiots can stay out here and catch pneumonia." The women dashed into the house. Betty shot Paul a hard look as she went inside.

"Ah hell, stay for another beer," Paul said.

"There isn't any more. How about a rematch?"

"No, my luck's gone. You'd kick my ass." The sky spit lightning, and thunder rolled across the hills. From inside the house came a shriek of laughter. Paul picked up the gold horseshoes and held them over his head. He looked up into the storm and banged the shoes together twice, impatient, then let out a howl. Paul spun around and the rain kept falling and lightning flashed, but it was far away and therefore useless.

State of Grace

He hands her the tomato juice and frowns.

"We're going to need more of this," he says. She pours what's left in the can into her glass and stirs it with the vodka.

"Whatever."

She takes a good drink and puts her glass on the table. It is the twenty-eighth of November, and word has come that her father is dying. His time left is counted in hours. When she was a girl, she sometimes went camping with her dad. Once he took her to a lake in Canada where they stayed for a week and fished and looked at birds. They skinny-dipped in the shallows, but nothing ugly happened.

She's thinking about that trip now as she picks up her drink and takes a good swallow.

"Do you like to fish?" she asks.

"I haven't fished in years."

She starts to cry. "That's not what I asked," she says.

"I guess I do," he says. "I guess I like to fish." He wants to hold her, but they have been arguing. Just before the phone call came about her father, they were arguing about a woman she is certain he is infatuated with. In truth, he is more than infatuated. He has been having a weekly rendezvous at the Blue Sky Motel with this woman for more than a month, but he has tried to be careful not to let it show. For whatever reason, he still loves his wife. The new woman is getting to be a problem, though. He has an awful feeling she might try to break up his marriage. She's had that tone, lately. He thinks she has called his house and hung up the phone more than once. The hang-ups only happen when his wife answers the phone.

He fears his life has become a cliché.

"We better get our things together and get moving," he says. "We better hurry if we're going to make it."

She takes another drink. For now, she has forgotten about the other woman. All she can think about is her father, six feet tall, muscular, naked in that Canadian lake. The thought of packing a suitcase, to travel across the country to see what is left of him, leaves her bewildered.

"I don't care about any of this," she says. She wonders silently if she has ever been more than that little girl, looking up at her father.

"What do you mean?" He studies her face, looking for an answer, but he can't pick up any clear signal.

She is thinking of a cold place and water.

"I wonder who you are," she says, reaching for his face. He presses his hand against hers. They sit like that in the living room, terrified. The phone begins to ring. "Oh, dear God," each of them thinks. "Not now."

Test Day

Lisa has red hair, blue eyes, and can't decide if she loves or hates the freckles on her face and arms. She definitely loves tuna sandwiches, though, and has one for lunch every day. Some days, Lisa's mom packs her lunchbox with a homemade brownie or a couple of chocolate chip cookies made from her grandmother's secret recipe. Lisa usually shares her desert with her best friend, Elizabeth, but Elizabeth is sick today and absent from school.

A boy who sits two rows over and one back has been in love with Lisa for at least a month, but she doesn't know this. She does know his name is Benjamin, however, and, like everyone, is secretly jealous of his ability to draw faces so real you can tell who they're supposed to be every time. Imagine her surprise if she ever saw the stacks of portraits he keeps hidden in his room: dozens of pictures of a girl with red hair, blue eyes, and constellations of freckles.

The room is filled with intrigues. Hidden loves, promises kept and broken, the standard sixth-grade stuff that most survive and, eventually, laugh about.

An eighth-grade boy, Michael, for reasons known only to himself, has brought a pistol to school today. The gun belongs to Michael's father, who keeps it, loaded, on the top shelf of his bedroom closet. In five minutes, Michael will open the door to Lisa and Benjamin's classroom and begin shooting randomly at the children. Lisa, along with two of her classmates, and Michael will die. But right now, right this second, Lisa is thinking about her best friend, Elizabeth, thinking how lucky she is to be home today. They are supposed to have a math test later, and Lisa is not ready.

Family Ties

I.

The last time I was at these waters I nearly drowned, but that was years ago, when I was a boy. I've learned to stay on the right side of the fence, and I stand here, safe, looking onto a shrinking horizon. The clouds are gathering in the distance, angry, gray, almost black. I can't worry about that.

I am here for the lie.

My daughter stands beside me. She's six months gone with child and unmarried. The man—the boy—who fathered the thing growing inside her ran like a whipped pup when he was told. Lisa refused to abort. We stand here, the two of us, watching and listening as the waves crash against the rocks, as the clouds gather and threaten.

"Daddy," she says, and puts her hand on mine. I let it rest there a moment and then, as gently as I can, move away. Lisa makes a noise in her throat as if she would say more, but no words come out. I put my hands in my pockets and am careful to look straight ahead.

"All hell's going to break loose, it looks like," I say. Lisa doesn't answer for a while. Then she says "Daddy," again. Daddy. I can feel the fear in her voice and let myself look at her. Her hair is wet from the spray, the waves punishing the rocks, and it is flattened against her head. In her loose jacket and slacks, it isn't noticeable that she is this pregnant. Anybody who didn't know probably wouldn't guess.

"Yes," I say. Lightning webs the sky in brilliant relief. For all its power, there is no anger to lightning.

I am here for the lie.

"I know Charlie will do right. I know he'll be back." She's looking at me, looking up at my chin. She can't meet my eyes, and I'm happy for that. "Daddy, it'll be okay."

"Yes," I say. "Everything will be fine." Lisa puts her arms around my waist and we stare together at the uncontrollable water, the dazed rocks, the lightning.

I was once a boy at this water, and I almost drowned, stepping into currents strong, uncaring, unknowable.

II.

The baby is a boy, and she names him Daniel, for me. Daniel was born with a full head of bushy, black hair. His eyes were blue at birth, but the doctor says they may change to brown. Lisa has quit school, dropped out for a year so she can stay home and take care of her son. She swears to me she will go back next year and finish.

I go to work every day; and when I come home, Lisa has supper ready. She's a good girl, no matter the awful thing she did. At home I sit in my room and read my Bible. Daniel cries most of the time, and Lisa does what she can to shush him. It sometimes works for a while, but then he starts up again. I read aloud to shut out the noise, the word of God ringing from my walls, drowning out the screams of sin rolling through my house like thunder.

III.

They found Charlie last night. He had been missing since April, since just after Lisa started to show. She didn't tell me about the baby until she began to put on weight, until she finally had to. Everyone figured Charlie had run off rather than face his responsibilities, that if he showed up at all it would be years later, or maybe there would eventually be a post card from New York or Omaha or someplace. They didn't expect to find him in the woods. The coroner said he'd been there for months from the look of things. It was his teeth that showed who he was. Dental records. That was their only hope. In the newspaper it says he died of a gunshot wound to the head.

IV.

Daniel is six months old. I remember the day he was born. Lisa was in labor for twelve hours. When she was born, her mother had labor for almost twenty-four. Women hold the pain of the world; and when they can no longer contain it, they scream it out. Else men would never know it is real. It has been more than two months since I saw my grandson. When Lisa went away, it was night. She left me a note telling me not to look for her; she and the baby would be fine.

I can't make sense of anything. My days tumble into one another, and I stare into them but see nothing but my four walls, the hard floors and ceilings.

The police were here asking questions. "There are no guns here," I told them. Presently, they left, but Lisa began looking at me strangely, and it wasn't too many mornings later that I found her note.

V.

First came the water. The rocks. The thunder and the lightning. I went back to the place where Lisa and I had stood, balanced on the edge of this sad tomorrow. I hoped to find some trace of her, but of course there was nothing. For hours I watched the ocean, calmer now, but still deadly in its indifference. Then came the road. I looked in the obvious places. The bars, the lounges of cheap motels. Street corners.

I have found Lisa many times, and many times I have made her pay. A father's love is unbounded. My grandson is hidden, but she will not say where. I will find her again, soon. Perhaps this time she will give me Daniel. I am sick of the lie. May the

Lord forgive my daughter. Heaven be merciful. Jesus saves. Amen.

Bonnie and Clyde

Martha hadn't seen Jim in almost five years, and now here he was, staring back at her from the front page of the morning paper. She was on her second cup of decaf. Her cup was almost empty, so she filled it again and then read the story under the photograph for the third time.

There had been a fire in a house on the north end, one of those shotgun houses, Martha figured, because that area was full of them and trashy, though the paper didn't say. What it did say was that a dog was trapped inside. Jim was walking past the house and saw a little girl screaming on the sidewalk. He'd run inside and saved the dog, a three-legged dachshund that lived inside because it was crippled. The child's mother was quoted as saying Jim was a real hero. Jim was in the hospital with second degree burns and smoke inhalation. The paper didn't mention a prognosis.

The photograph was too perfect. It looked like it was from a studio. To Martha, it looked like Jim had looked five years before. There was no telling when it was taken or how the paper had gotten hold of it.

She put the paper on the table and was sipping from her cup when Tom came downstairs. He was already dressed in his usual uniform: khaki trousers, white shirt and burgundy tie, Windsor knot. He wore his tan, corduroy jacket with the suede elbow patches. Martha got his bowl and cereal and milk and set them on the table, then got his coffee. He fixed his cereal and took a bite before picking up the paper.

"Son of a bitch," he said. "Did you see this?"

"Yes," she said.

"That is Bill and Edna's son, isn't it? What the hell's he doing here?

"I don't know."

"Have you called them?"

"No."

Tom took a big bite of toasted oats and crunched it as he read the story.

"Says he got burned up to save a dog. Jesus."

"I know."

Tom finished his breakfast at eight o'clock and left for school. It was a three-quarter mile walk, which took him exactly twenty minutes. That gave him ten minutes to check his mail and straighten his tie before the morning lecture. On his way out he told Martha he'd surely see Bill or Edna and would find out what he could about Jim. Tom said he'd call if he heard anything.

Martha cleaned up the dishes and picked up the paper again. She examined the photo closely. The eyes were just as she remembered.

Martha met Jim when they were both in graduate school. She was studying to be a librarian. Library work suited her exactly. She loved the order and beauty of the Dewey Decimal System. The rows of neatly and correctly shelved books gave her an anchor, a stable world in which to take root, flourish. She had a graduate assistantship in the reference room, and every day at lunch time she walked over to the student union for a peach yogurt and Tab. On this particular day, she was alone in the cafeteria at high noon and every other table was filled. A dark, shaggy-haired man in his late twenties walked over and asked if he could sit down with his burger and fries. Martha thought he was cute.

"Suit yourself," she said. Martha was reading a book which her roommate, Debbie, had asked her to return to the library. It was *Quiet Days in Clichy*, and Martha had been marveling at how something this dirty could ever get published. The man sat down and took a bite of his burger.

"Henry Miller," he said. "Great book."

"Uh huh," she said, then raised her eyes above the book. He looked all right—thick black hair that just needed cutting, clear blue eyes. He almost looked familiar, but she couldn't quite place him. Probably she had seen him around campus, but there was something else, too. Something a little thrilling, a little danger inside the eyes. But not too much, really. Really, he seemed okay.

So Martha and Jim became friends. She found out he was working on a doctorate in English and was trying to write. That seemed exciting to her in some vague way. They went out a few times, but when Debbie grilled her on the romance, she insisted it was no big deal.

They slept together after their third date. They'd been to a revival of *Bonnie and Clyde* at the campus cinema, and after the movie they went to Lynagh's for drinks. After two Long Island teas, Martha felt dangerous. It hit her then, who Jim looked like. He looked like Clyde Barrow, or maybe it was only Warren Beatty, but whichever, she liked it. She felt the wind in her hair, the thrill of a Tommy gun chugging bullets into bright wonder and night. She slipped off her shoe and ran her black-stockinged toes up Jim's leg.

They went to Jim's apartment. On the drive over, Martha was almost giddy. Through the whole encounter, bullets and Faye and Warren whizzed inside her brain. A few days later she realized her period was late. She sweated it out for the better part of a week before, finally, she bled. After that, Martha and Jim began seeing less and less of one another. When Jim asked her out, she came up with excuses but didn't tell him the real reason, her simple fear of disorder.

Something about Jim made her forget the tight, tidy life she was preparing, and she didn't like it. By the time Martha graduated, she saw Jim only when they bumped into each other in the library. Jim was just beginning his dissertation when Martha walked down the aisle in her cap and gown to pick up her degree.

The last time Martha and Jim were together was back in 1988. By one of those funny coincidences, Martha had landed a job at the college where Jim's parents taught. She'd been there about a year when Jim was given a summer appointment to teach Composition. Something had gone wrong, or maybe just got delayed, but Jim wasn't in the Ph.D. program anymore. By the time he got there, Martha was already second in command at the library, and a member of the college's building funds committee. She was also seeing Tom, an up-and-coming History professor with a Subaru.

She was glad to see Jim, though, and made a point to phone him to make sure they got together. On evenings when Tom was busy, she'd call up Jim, and they'd go out for drinks. She didn't bother to tell Jim about Tom, or vice versa. After all, they were only friends, and Tom wasn't quite nailed down yet. It was one of those evenings out for drinks that Jim gave her that stare. Martha had on a silky black dress, a flimsy little thing she knew looked good on her. Martha liked being looked at, but this was something else. Jim's gaze was penetrating, but that didn't really describe it. It was something more than that, and it made her uneasy. Jim had his beer in his hand and he was talking about something, she couldn't remember what, and his eyes were fixed on hers.

"Stop it," she said. "You're looking way too intense."

She felt something working in her belly, something deep and ticklish. It was more than just sex, and it almost felt good, but mostly it just scared her. That night when Jim dropped her off, he tried to kiss her, but she pulled away.

"I like you," she said. "But I don't feel comfortable with this." She got out of the car fast. He reached for her and got the shoulder of her dress. She kept moving and the fabric ripped halfway down her left breast, exposing the black bra underneath. Martha stopped and moved back into the car. Jim still held her dress.

"Go ahead, tear it," she said. Martha's heart was beating so hard that it hurt. Her breath came in gulps, and it was difficult for her to get the words out.

She put her hand on his and squeezed hard. She pulled it so the fabric ripped again, another six inches. Jim took both of her breasts in his hands and caressed them.

"Oh, God," she said.

She began slapping him, hitting his face and arms. She raked her nails across his cheek and jumped from the car. Jim didn't try to stop her. Inside her house she lay on her bed and couldn't stop shaking.

It was near the end of the summer, and Jim didn't drop by the library anymore, and Martha didn't call him out for drinks. Jim managed to land a job in Georgia and left as soon as the term was over. From time to time Edna, Jim's mother, dropped by the library to gossip with Doris, the head librarian, about their mutual friends and enemies. She occasionally had word from Jim. A poem published here, a story there, some small triumph painted large. Martha always tried to sound interested, because Edna was a full professor and good friends with Doris, but she just didn't much care. There was a residual grudge over the dress and what she now considered practically a rape, though she never mentioned the incident to anyone. Also, by this time she'd snared Tom. Within a year after Jim moved on, Martha and Tom were married.

Tom was already comfortable when they first met. He had his doctorate from the University of Pittsburgh, his specialty the Crimean War. Tom knew all there was to know about the Crimean war, and he told charming anecdotes about the generals and their important battles. He was an active member of the town's historical society and had a large collection of memorabilia from several wars, including flags and insignia, medals—even a few guns and knives. He also had money he'd inherited from an aunt and was secure in his position at the college. His wavy hair and broad shoulders made him look a good deal more interesting than he actually was. There were flocks of eighteen-year-old girls who hovered around him, taking his classes and constantly coming by his office to discuss the Crimean War or other things, but Martha had little trouble fending them off.

They settled. Martha kept her job for the first three years, then she got pregnant and quit. Tom wasn't the most exciting husband in the world, but he had a good job and money. He would make a good father. They never fought except over the occasional slight Tom believed he suffered. To both of their surprise, it turned out he was quite jealous and often brooded about the attention Martha got from the few young men who hung around the library. Once, before she became pregnant, Tom slapped Martha during an argument in which she denied flirting with a sophomore boy who paid his tuition with work study in the library. He slapped her hard, and she was sure he was going to hit her again, but instead he turned red and started crying. Martha left for a week but came home when she couldn't stand the Blue Sky Motel any longer. Tom bought her a new car and told her he'd never hit her again. Except for another time when he got mad about a different kid showing her some attention at school, Tom kept his word. That time, Martha made Tom leave and didn't let him come home for almost a month.

But things had been running smoothly in the few months before the pregnancy. They were as happy as they had ever been. The baby was almost full-term when she miscarried, and complications made it unlikely she would ever be able to have another chance. The doctor advised her not to go back to work for a while. Martha and Tom had been talking about her getting another library job soon, but she secretly welcomed the doctor's warning. More and more the rows and stacks of books and magazines were losing their luster. Rather than a safe haven they now seemed almost unbearable. They were too quiet, too dead. She offered token resistance and then agreed to stay at home a while.

It was after the miscarriage that she began thinking of Jim. She was at home by herself one afternoon, sitting in the kitchen, when his face flashed inside her. It was that face from the last night she saw him. It still scared her, but she couldn't seem to get it out of her mind. For days that face kept popping into her head, those blue eyes staring straight at her. The eyes were dangerous. This was months before the picture in the newspaper.

Of course, Martha never mentioned anything to Tom. After a while, Jim began to seem more real than her actual life. By this time she had begun to pull into herself and away from her husband. Despite Tom's jealousy, their sex life had never been particularly passionate or important to either of them, but now Martha actively resisted Tom's occasional advances. Sometimes she made an excuse, and sometimes she didn't bother. Day to day life passed much as it always had though, and somehow that made it seem so much worse. She often found herself thinking about that night in the car with Jim. Maybe it was her fault. Maybe it had been a huge blunder. She began to think this was the one major error in her life, the one wrong turn from which there was no way back.

***

All morning she puttered around the house, thinking of reasons Jim might be in town. Nothing made sense, least of all that he was there for her, but she just couldn't get the idea out of her mind. By the time she left the house, she had convinced herself that Jim, at the very least, would be dying to see her. She kept thinking about his eyes.

117

Martha got to the hospital around one o'clock. She hadn't planned at all on going, but here she was. She got Jim's room number from the front desk—room 308—and went on up. The door was slightly ajar, but she still knocked before stepping inside.

"Come in," said a voice.

She went in. There was Jim in the bed, wearing a hospital gown. He looked about the same as always, except that now he had a beard. He looked at her as if he didn't know her.

"Well, hello there," she said brightly. "If it isn't the hero. Oh my God, how are you? Are you burned up?" She was babbling, and she knew it, but she couldn't stop. "And here you are, back in town and the first thing you do is almost kill yourself. I swear."

"Hello, Martha," Jim said. Then he said, "I sure didn't expect to see you here."

Martha made it as close as the foot of the bed and then stopped. She stood there and fidgeted, and for a long moment neither of them said anything.

"Well, pull up a chair," Jim finally said. "What brings you out this way?"

"What brings? Why you, silly. You and that dog you saved. It's in the paper, the whole story. I had to come over and see how you were."

"I'm fine. I had some burns—hands, arms, legs." He held up his arms to illustrate. "And smoke inhalation. I passed out, so they brought me here for observation. I think they'll let me go in a day or two."

Martha nodded. Then, unable to think of anything else to say, she stood abruptly and blurted, "Okay, I just wanted to say hello. Make sure you don't leave town without giving me a call, all right?"

"Sure."

She hadn't looked him full in the face until then. Now she did and there were those eyes. Perhaps they sort of resembled Clyde Barrow or Warren Beatty, but mostly they looked tired,

118

maybe a little confused. She held his gaze for a second and felt like she should say something else. What she thought she should say was, "I'm sorry," but she didn't for the life of her know why.

"Why'd you do that for a dog?" was what she said.

"Sometimes you don't think; you just do."

She had a sudden urge to kiss him, to swallow him up and run away to someplace hot and secret. What she said was, "A goddamn three-legged dog."

***

The little red light on the answering machine was flashing when Martha walked into her kitchen. She pushed the button and Jim's voice said, "Hello? Hello? Honey, are you there?" Martha blushed when she realized it was actually Tom.

***

When Tom got home from the college, he was met with the smell of pork chops and mashed potatoes, his favorite dinner. He wasn't quite through with his meal before Martha was rubbing his back and chest and breathing in his ear. Tom tried to go on with the last of his chops, but Martha was persistent. She bit him and whispered hard, "Now, goddamn it. Right now." They started in the dining room and finished in bed. Every time Tom finished he tried to go to sleep, but Martha wouldn't let him. She cajoled or bullied him into compliance until finally, somewhere in the small, black hours before daylight, she said "Enough." Tom rolled over and dozed off, and Martha watched the slowly gathering light until sleep finally took her, too. She dreamed of cleansing flame and children and crippled dogs. Somehow, they all seemed involved in a great battle, with generals and soldiers and even spies and grand intrigue. At the end was a 1920s Ford cruising two-lanes and dusty back roads, racing fast toward nowhere special. It seemed to make sense at the time, but in the

119

morning, there was just a jumble of images that she barely remembered.

That was the night before the day Tom's historical society met. He and a group of men got together one day a month to relive old wars and show off relics. Just that week Tom had tracked down a WWII British Special Forces dagger, in almost mint condition. He placed it inside his briefcase that morning before walking to work. Jim showed up in the afternoon. It was just past three o'clock when Martha answered the knock at the front door, and there he stood. He had on shorts and a tee-shirt, and his calves and forearms were wrapped in gauze.

"Hello," he said.

Martha stared at him for a second and then said hello back.

"What brings you here?" she asked.

"Oh, just thought I'd stop by to say hello. If you're busy—"

"No, of course not. Come on in."

They sat down in the living room. Martha sat on the couch, and Jim took the recliner. She stretched out her legs and crossed them. Her skirt lay a few inches above her knee.

"I can't really stay long," he said. "I'm on my way to visit the Shepherds, and then I'm off to Georgia."

"The Shepherds?"

"The people whose house burned down. I want to see how the dog's doing. Pretty screwed up way to celebrate my parent's anniversary, eh?"

"Your parents?" She took a deep breath and let it out slowly, her cheeks burning. Martha had all but convinced herself that Jim was back in town for her, and it was a shock to think he could be here for any other reason.

"Thirty-five years. I hardly got to see them with all this mess." There was half a pot of coffee left over from breakfast and Martha poured them each a cup. They shared small talk as they sipped their cups, and when he finished his coffee, Jim said he'd better go.

Three blocks away, Tom was walking home angry. His classes hadn't gone particularly well, and then the historical society meeting had been canceled. Dr. Campbell had the flu, and two of the others pleaded last minute conflicts. Tom hated being stood up, and the more he thought about it, the madder he got. It was like they didn't respect him, and he hated that. He felt like hitting someone; that was how he felt. Tom had been dying to show off his new dagger, which still rode, within easy reach, inside his briefcase.

Jim stood and Martha got up from the couch and walked with him to the door. Before he could open it she put her hand on his. "I had the strangest idea," she said. She squeezed his hand, then put it on her shoulder. "If there's anything you want. If there's anything." She moved his hand to her breast and left it there and then put her hands, lightly, on his waist. Her voice trailed off and there they stood, two outlaws. Martha knew that Tom was ten thousand miles away fighting the Crimean War, and she hung inside that moment, waiting for an answer.

On the Brink

"Hey, pass the sugar."

I hand him the sugar. It's in one of those tall, glass dispensers with a metal top and a little flap for the sugar to go through, the kind of thing you don't see much of anymore. Hell, who uses sugar these days? It's all those dietary things in the pink and blue packets. Awful. Not Teddy, though. He still goes in for the real thing.

Teddy pours the sugar into his coffee without measuring it. He pours for about a second and then swirls it around with his spoon. He takes a big drink and then he continues.

"So, there we were," he says, "cruising Third Street, looking for whores. We see this black woman on the corner and Ray pulls off. He rolls down his window, and she walks on over. We're really drunk, sure, but I remember she had—"

The phone rings while he's telling me this. Marcia picks it up on the second ring then hollers over at me, interrupting Teddy's story.

"Hey, Billy, it's your wife. She wants you to come home."

I nod at Marcia and wave, then shrug at Teddy.

"Gotta go. We'll finish this one next time, okay?"

I can see that Teddy is disappointed he didn't get to finish his story. He spends a lot of time thinking about things he's done, or things he wishes he had done, and then he tells me about them. We like to sit in the third booth from the door, right beside a window, and drink coffee. We meet on Thursday nights and drink our coffee, and Teddy tells me his stories. But things got off to a slow start tonight, and by the time Teddy was cooking, Beth was on the phone telling Marcia it was time I trot back to the house. She didn't use to care if I stayed out late on Thursdays, because she knew exactly where I was, that there was no drinking, no fooling around with other women. I think she even liked Teddy. Sometimes I'd come home, and she would still be awake, and I'd crawl into bed with her and tell her the story Teddy had told me that night. That must have happened a dozen times, and I liked it a lot when it did. It gave me a chance to live through the story again, and, when I did it right, I believe it gave Beth the same feeling I had had listening to Teddy.

But lately things have changed. The thing is, Beth is pregnant. She's late into the eighth month now and hates to have me gone very long. I don't blame her one bit. Anything could happen. So many bad accidents happen right in the home. The kitchen, especially, and I hear the bathroom is bad, too. So it's not good for Beth to putter around the house by herself, not this late in the game. Plus, I guess she gets lonely. I know she's happy to be pregnant, but I can look at her face sometimes and know she's scared. I try to tell her everything will be fine, but I don't think she always believes me.

So I go home. My old VW has been acting up some, but it hasn't let me down yet. There's a miss in the engine, and I figure it's probably the plugs. I know very little about cars, but I've decided it's the spark plugs. I keep meaning to take her into the shop, but I just haven't found the time yet.

I park on the street and notice lights are on in the living room. Inside I find her there on the couch, lying down, the phone within easy reach on the coffee table. She's asleep. I wake her by kissing her on each eye.

"What time is it?" she asks.

"About ten. I came home as soon as you called."

"Oh. Thanks. I started getting a little afraid. You don't mind, do you?"

"Of course not. Come on, let's get ready for bed." I help Beth off the couch, and we walk down the hall toward the bedroom. On the way we pass the bathroom and she needs to stop.

"I won't be long," she says.

"Right."

I wait in the bedroom. She's out in ten minutes, and I go in and brush my teeth and pee. By the time I'm finished, Beth is already in bed, waiting. I climb in beside her and turn out the light.

"How was it tonight?" she asks.

"It was okay. He didn't really finish the story."

Beth starts to cry. It seems like lately the slightest thing sets her off. "It's my fault, isn't it? I called and made you come home early. I'm so sorry." By the time she gets to "sorry," she's crying so hard that it comes out in four syllables. I put my arms around her and shush into her neck.

"No, no. It's not your fault. He just got started late. It didn't seem like one of his better efforts anyway."

Beth calms a little, and I hold her lightly in my arms. She feels better than anything in this world has a right to feel next to me. I love her big belly between us, our baby swimming around inside.

"What was it about?"

"All he got to was something about cruising around in a car with a buddy of his. He hadn't gotten to the story part yet."

"Well, maybe that's better than him getting halfway into it and leaving you hanging. It's a good thing I didn't call five minutes later, huh?"

"I guess it is." I kiss her neck and then her mouth. She moans a little and moves closer to me. He breasts are twice their normal size and tender. I touch her, letting my hands caress her breasts, her belly. Making love is awkward, but the doctor said it would be fine until quite late in the pregnancy.

"Oh, Billy," she says. She keeps saying my name, and I lose myself into this woman and this child.

124

The next morning Beth is sick, vomiting in the bathroom. I've learned that there isn't much I can do, other than offer moral support and do my best to keep the house picked up. I also do a lot of the cooking these days, though that isn't my strong suit. While Beth cleans herself up, I go into the kitchen and fix her some cereal and half a grapefruit, then I head back to the bathroom.

"You okay?"

"Fine, better."

"Your breakfast is on the table. I have to go."

"Okay, sweetie. Thanks. Have a good day." She hugs and kisses me. I start to leave and she asks a question:

"Do you love me?"

I walk back and hug her. "More than anything," I say.

"I love you."

"I know."

She brightens, and I make it out the door. Traffic isn't too bad, so I make it to work a couple of minutes early. I'm a librarian. I work the reference desk at the public library, and since I'm early I have a quick cup of coffee before I tidy things up, make sure the computers are turned on and there are enough pencils for patrons to copy down call numbers. Then I open the door and let the early birds in. There are only two today, a couple of women, and we say good morning to each other as they come inside.

It's a slow day, and I like that. Sometimes things get so hectic around here that I can't imagine why I ever went into this line of work. Then I remember: It's better than teaching, which is what I did before I went back to school for my MLS. No papers to grade, no irate parents to deal with. Yes, this is better. Since it is a slow day, my mind wanders. I keep flashing back to Teddy's story. I can see him, young and nervous, pulling over to negotiate with a hooker. I remember that he said he had a friend with him, but in my mind I only see Teddy pulling off and buying the woman's services. I'm thinking about this and becoming aroused

125

when Mrs. Marstin, one of our regulars, walks up to the reference desk and asks me if I'll help her find a book on the care of tropical fish.

"Of course," I say, and walk out onto the floor, trying to keep my erection from being noticeable.

After work, I head right home. Beth is lying on the couch watching *Jeopardy*. She watches it every night and always gets a lot of answers right. I kid her sometimes that she should become a contestant.

"Hi, sweetie," she says. "How was your day?"

I bend down and kiss her. "Oh, you know."

That night I have dreams. I dream I'm in a whorehouse. The walls are crushed red velvet and there are women everywhere dressed in lingerie or miniskirts with see-through tops, or just naked. There's an old fashioned piano in the corner, and some guy plays a fast blues number. The music eludes me. Then another woman appears, a black woman. She has on a maternity dress, but it opens in front so I can see her private parts. Her arms are open and beckoning. I go to her and put my arms around her and kiss her, squeezing her breasts in my hands.

"Ouch, ow, you're hurting me!" It's Beth. I've rolled close to her and have been squeezing her sensitive breasts. I'm instantly awake.

"Honey, I'm sorry. I was dreaming about you."

"Really? That's so sweet, but I'm awfully tired. Can we do this some other time?"

"Yes. Yeah, of course. You go back to sleep." Beth closes her eyes. In minutes I hear her breath get slow and deep. I lie in the dark for a long time before I'm able to drift off.

Beth is sick again in the morning. Same old routine. I fix her breakfast and kiss her. Before I can leave she says, "Sorry about last night."

"You remember that?"

"Barely. I thought for a minute that it was a dream, but then I noticed these scratches on my breasts. You were pretty hot."

"Oops. Sorry. Are you okay?"

"I'm fine, but you'd better be ready for tonight."

"Sounds like a challenge."

"Consider yourself warned."

I gently squeeze her left nipple and then I'm out the door. All day at work I'm in a state of arousal. I think of Beth, and I get hard. Then my mind wanders. I remember my dream, and then I think about cruising Third Street looking for whores. I mean I think of Teddy doing this. At least I tell myself this is what I mean. It's hard for me to keep my eyes off my co-workers, even though none of them are very pretty. Beth calls them a bunch of old maids, and she's right. But the way I feel right now, the very femaleness of them, how much ever there is, is dangerous.

At home that night Beth greets me in the bedroom. The lights are off, and she's burning candles. She is wearing a sexy red maternity gown, all lace and gauze and ruffles. It's all I can do to not simply attack her, rape her. In the midst of things, between moans of passion, she has to remind me to go easy.

"Remember the baby, Billy. Careful—"

***

And then another day at work. I steal glances at the other librarians, at the women and girls who wander in looking for books. I want them all. Of course I have allowed myself glances before. Married, not dead, that's me. But this is different. There is something wild inside me. I feel powerful, virile, invincible.

I call Beth at four o'clock and tell her I'll be a little late because we are having a staff meeting, and I can't get out of it. She understands. Then I tell Mrs. Green, the library director, that I am not feeling well and ask if it would be okay if I go home early.

"Sure, Bill," she says. "We'll manage."

127

I do all of this without planning to. The idea just came over me that I needed to get out of there, needed to have some free time with nobody expecting me to show up at a given moment. But, truth to tell, I am not surprised when I find myself on the north end of town, the bad section. I drive slowly, looking at the houses, the stores. There are a lot of black men hanging around. The only women I see look like mothers, like respectable women. There are a couple of shopping cart ladies, too, one of them obviously insane, talking loudly to herself as she pushes her cart along the sidewalk. But I don't see anybody who looks like a whore.

Beth is in bed when I get home, but not asleep. There is nothing of last night's seduction about her now. She has on an old pair of my flannel pajamas, and the cover is tucked under her chin. She doesn't look like she feels very well.

"How was your meeting?"

"Fine. Boring. Awful. You know how those things are."

"Poor baby."

"Thanks."

My days and nights begin to blur. I sleep that night and work the next day, then sleep and work again. In between I cook for Beth and try to keep the house neat and comfort her when she is sick. Sunday rolls around, and we lounge around the house all day. I am so in love with Beth that it hurts. She seems to be getting more and more uncomfortable, but otherwise everything is fine. Everything is great.

That's why I can't explain the thing about the hooker. I simply can't get rid of the idea of paying a strange woman to have sex with me. It all goes back to Teddy's story, I suppose. He put the idea into my head. A whore. A black whore. What in life could be better?

Tuesday night I go out driving. I tell Beth I need to get out for a while and drive, maybe drive over to the park and walk for a while. The stress, I say. The stress of my job is killing me. She says she understands.

"Take your time," she says as I walk out the door. "I'll be fine."

I climb into the car feeling like a traitor, but that doesn't stop me from driving to the north end of town. I figure I was probably too early when I went before. The working girls must come out at night.

I cruise maybe five minutes before I see a girl who is obviously on the make. I pull up to the curb and roll down my window.

"Looking for a date?" she says.

"How much?" I have never done anything remotely like this in my life.

"What do you want?"

"Oh, the usual."

She laughs.

"Honey, I don't know what's usual for you. Tell me what you want, and I'll tell you the price."

"Just sex. Just a regular fuck." That last word is difficult to say and now I'm embarrassed.

"That would be fifty dollars cash." I pull out my wallet and count the money, hand it to her. She reaches into her purse and pulls out a gun and badge.

"Okay, pal, you're under arrest. Get out of the car now." Two men appear from nowhere, more cops. They handcuff me and read me my rights, and the next thing I know I'm in a police car on my way to jail. When they get me there, they fingerprint me and take my picture and tell me I can go home if someone will come and post a hundred dollars bail.

I am frantic. There is no way in the world I can call Beth. Hi honey, I just got arrested for soliciting a prostitute. Could you and our unborn child come down to the police station and bail my sorry ass out of here? Yeah, right.

So I call Teddy. I'm not sure he'll be listed, but he is and I call him up.

"Teddy? It's Billy. Listen, have you got a hundred dollars? I'm in some trouble." But Teddy doesn't have a hundred dollars. He doesn't have twenty. I know there is no one else to call. I can't let Beth worry about me all night, not with her this pregnant. I swallow hard and ask Teddy to call Beth for me. That one phone call business and all.

"What do I tell her?"

"Tell her it was a DUI."

"Will she believe it?"

"I don't know. I just don't know."

An hour later a cop comes by and opens my cell, says I've made bail. Beth is waiting for me in the lobby. She has obviously been crying. She won't look at me. She has come to the police station in a taxi and changed from her gown into daytime maternity clothes. She looks beautiful. The cops give me my keys and wallet and we walk out and find my car where they parked it. Beth still hasn't spoken a word. We get into the car.

"How could you do this?" she says.

"I just had a couple of beers—"

"Don't lie. Just don't lie to me anymore. The police told me why you were arrested."

I feel like I am on fire.

"Beth, honey. It's not what you think. The whole thing was a misunderstanding. A mistake." I rush my words. I know she sees the lies.

"I can't talk about this now," she says. "Let's just go home. Tomorrow I'm going to my mother's house and stay there till after the baby comes. After that, I don't know."

"Beth—"

"Will you please shut up? Will you please not say a word?"

We get home, and Beth goes right to bed. I sleep on the couch. I wake up the next morning right after dawn, the doorbell ringing me awake. It is Elaine, Beth's mother. Beth is already packed and ready. Elaine is furious. I suppose it is taking all of her self-control to keep her from physically attacking me. She marches her daughter out of the house as quickly and efficiently as possible.

"I'll call you," I say to Beth as she walks by me. She doesn't answer.

"Beth will call you," Elaine says, "when she's ready." Then they are gone. I walk into the bedroom. Beth has made the bed, the first time she has done that in weeks. I pull back the covers and bury my face in her pillow, searching for her smell. I find it and breathe deeply, holding the air in my lungs. I think about calling in sick, but I know the worst thing I can do is sit around the house all day thinking about what has happened.

Things go excruciatingly slowly at the library, but finally, somehow, the work day ends. When I get home, I lie down for a while in the bedroom. The phone rings and I answer right away.

"Beth?"

"It's me, Billy. It's Teddy. Listen, sorry about last night, but I'm broke. We still on for tonight? I imagine you have a story or two to tell this time, eh?"

I sit there with the receiver in my hand, no idea what to say. After a minute I hear Teddy again. "Hello? Hello? You there?" I have the funny feeling that I am not. I hang up the phone. That's all I can think to do. Then I have an overpowering thought. "I'm going to be a daddy," I say. Then I say it louder. And then the room is quiet.

Frank's Bad Day

The old man tugged her sleeve and then pinched her on the bottom. Lucy turned halfway around and caught him a good one with her purse, smack on the left ear.

"Oh sweet Jesus," he said.

"I've had it, Frank."

"Come on, baby, cut me some slack."

They sat there at the bar and drank their drinks. After a while the bartender wandered over and asked if they needed another round. He'd seen what went between them before, but it was old news. These two were regulars.

"Fill 'er up, Jerome. Lucy?"

"I don't know. You behave?"

Frank ignored her.

"Lucy, too," he said.

Jerome wandered off to fix two martinis, not very dry, with cocktail onions.

"See, as I was saying, this would be good for us. A little fresh blood."

Lucy snorted. Frank had been trying to convince her to try a three way with the widow Jessup for the past two months. He'd been hot for Ruby Jessup for a while, but especially so ever since her late husband, Larry, the man with a crooked spine, fell into the grinder down at the dog food company. Lucy wasn't biting.

"Fresh what?" She sneered over her shoulder at him as Jerome set their drinks on the bar and wandered away again.

"You have a dirty mind."

"You're a filthy little creep."

Frank sighed. Ruby was a handsome woman, not much past sixty, and he had had his eye on her for years. When Larry got ground up, he thought maybe he'd get his chance. Then he got scruples and decided to ask Lucy to come in on the deal. That was a big mistake.

The door to the street opened, and light soaked into the dead mahogany bar. Nobody looked up from their drink. A tall, sick looking man of forty-five walked over and sat down beside Frank.

"Whassup?" the man said.

"Just trying to show Lucy a good time."

Lucy blew air from her mouth in an action just south of a snide laugh.

"Don't pay any attention, Bruce. You know how she gets."

"This man bothering you, Ma?"

"He always bothers me, honey. What you doing in here? You s'pose to be workin'."

"I'm takin' the day off. I just come in here lookin' for Frank and you. I got something to talk to Frank about."

"I don't have any money."

"Did I ask?"

"You were about to."

"If that's the way you're gonna be, forget it. I'll see who else wants to get in on the action." Frank looked at Bruce and raised his eyebrows. He had never liked Lucy's son, and any action he had was probably shit. He listened because he was still hoping Lucy would come over to his way of thinking about the Jessup woman, and maybe he'd raise the chance of that by hearing out her stupid son.

"So?" he said.

"So guess what somebody left in my cab."

"A used rubber?"

"Fuck you, asshole. Forget—"

133

"Now you two watch your mouths," Lucy said. "Frank, be nice. Bruce, you tell us what somebody left in your cab."

Bruce pouted for a moment, then reached into his pants pocket and produced a small box. He looked around the bar to make sure he wasn't being watched, then he flipped open the lid. Inside was an old coin, big as a half-dollar, with odd foreign symbols on it, and a bag of white powder. The coin looked ancient. The bag seemed to be filled with cocaine.

"Well looky here," said Frank. "Shit."

"Damn straight," said Bruce.

"What is that? Son, what is that?"

Bruce glanced around the bar to make sure nobody was eavesdropping. Jerome was down at the end of the counter polishing a glass. The two other patrons were old men who looked like they didn't even know where they were.

"It's drugs, Mama," he whispered. "Cocaine, I'm pretty sure. And this coin looks like it's worth something, too. Look at this shit."

"And just what do you plan to do with it?"

"I'm gonna sell it. This stuff is worth money."

"Boy, you don't know your ass from a bowling alley, but you're lucky you found me here. You don't want to do nothing stupid with this stuff. This stuff get you sent up the river." Frank fingered the bag. There must have been an ounce of powder in there. "I'll tell you what, you want me to get rid of this for you? We split the profit fifty-fifty?"

"Looks like I should get more, since I found it."

"But I'm taking all the risk. But hell, you do it yourself if that's how you feel." Frank knew Bruce well enough to understand he would never have a clue how to get rid of either the coke or the coin. He took a good sip from his martini and stared straight ahead.

"Okay, fifty-fifty. When you gonna do it?"

"No time like right now. I'll go see what I can do." Frank scooped up the box and stuffed it in his coat. "This may take a

134

while. I'll be home when I can, Sugar." He kissed Lucy on the cheek and winked at Bruce. "I'll call you when I sell this stuff," he said.

Frank didn't bother to call ahead at Ruby Jessup's apartment. She lived over on Eighth Street, near the slaughterhouse. Frank wondered idly whether it bothered her to live so near to a place where animals were cut up after what had happened to her husband.

She answered the door in her bathrobe.

"Ruby, I've come to pay my respects."

"Hello, Frank. Where's Lucy?"

"She's visiting her niece. Mind if I come in?"

"I guess it's okay."

Ruby sat on the couch and motioned for Frank to take the easy chair. It was an overstuffed recliner that had belonged to Larry. The seat was mashed down where Larry had sat in it all those years. The back cushion was compressed at an odd angle. Frank figured it was because of Larry's crooked spine. Doreen's robe opened a bit as she sat down, and Frank caught a good look at her legs.

"So, how are things? You been doing okay?"

"It's tough, Frank. You know how it is."

"Yeah, I know. Things get hard, Ruby." He winked at her and pulled the box from his coat. "I brought you a little present to make you feel better." Frank opened the box and pulled out the bag of white powder. He held it up for her to see.

"Oh, my."

Frank opened the baggy and poured a small pile into his hand.

"Here you go."

Ruby stared at Frank's hand, then looked at his face.

"Are you crazy?"

"This is good shit. Come on, Ruby."

"You leave now, Frank."

"Hey, baby."

135

"Just go."

Frank held his hand to his face and inhaled deeply. He felt the rush hit hard and then he felt his heart seize up. Frank clutched his chest then fell straight forward, dead before his face hit the floor. Ruby sat in her chair and screamed. When she finally stood her robe flew open, and her hairy legs, which she had been about to shave when Frank knocked at the door, caught the air and gave her a shiver. She dialed 911, but flushed the powder before the paramedics arrived. The coin she stuck in her jewelry box which she hid in the closet.

Bruce and his mother waited at the bar for more than two hours. Bruce was getting nervous when the door finally opened at a quarter to five. He hoped it would be Frank, but instead it was Orville DeBiachi, down from Jersey, Bruce's last fare before he found the box in his cab and decided to take the rest of the day off.

"I forgot something in the taxi," Orville said. "You find a little box?"

Bruce shook his head and took a draw on his cigarette. He was too scared to say anything.

"You sure about that? I mean, this was a little box about yea big. Meant a lot to me."

Bruce kept his eyes front and his mouth tight. Anybody could have seen he was lying. Orville grabbed Bruce by the collar and shook him. Lucy, till this point minding her own business, yelled for Orville to get off Bruce. When he didn't, she screamed louder, then grabbed a bottle and hit him in the face. Orville, madder than ever, pulled a knife from his pocket and showed it to Bruce.

"You're a dead man unless you have something to give me." He was bleeding from his cheek. There was something in his eye that said he wasn't joking.

Eighty miles away, in Trenton, New Jersey, Mrs. Angeline DeBiachi was thinking about her husband. It was their anniversary, and she was sure he was planning something special.

Orville's gifts were never routine. She'd hinted that she wanted the heroin, but Orville was just nutty enough that she was never sure what she was going to get. Sometimes he got her knick knacks when she expected gold. He should have been home hours ago. She knew he always wanted a *ménage a trios* and her friend Gloria wouldn't wait around all day.

Showdown at the 7-Eleven

Midge and Jake decided to hold up the 7-Eleven. Midge needed money for her eye surgery, and Jake didn't have any money, so they decided to hold up the store and then check her into a hospital. No big deal. The 7-Eleven was on Third Street, right between the new McDonalds and Lester's Funeral Parlor. They called it the new McDonalds because it had only been there three years. There had been a stink a few years ago when convenience stores and fast food places started to go up around the funeral home, but now people pretty much took it in stride. They'd had the services for Midge's grandmother at Lester's back in 1993, and afterwards she and her brother had walked over to the 7-Eleven and bought a six pack and drank it, right there in the parking lot.

That was in the days when Midge and Lance were screwing. They were brother and sister, but they shared an apartment and slept in the same bed and screwed like minks. They'd been going at it ever since they were twelve years old. They were fraternal twins and looked nothing alike. The only family they had was their grandmother, and she was so old that she never came to visit, so they didn't have to even keep up a pretense of separate bedrooms. Nobody bothered them, and they were happy.

Everything came crashing down one day when Midge came home from her job at the slaughterhouse and found Lance with Fat Mary, the neighbor from down the hall. Midge had noticed Mary eyeing Lance for a long time, but Mary was so fat and ugly she knew Lance would never go for her. Mary worked as an attendant at the city morgue, and Midge and Lance used to joke about how the only man she was likely to get would be a customer. Besides, Midge knew she and Lance loved each other. When Midge came in the door—she was two hours early because an FDA man had surprised the plant with an inspection and found enough health hazards to shut the place down—Lance and Fat Mary were sitting on the couch drinking whiskey. Lance's pants were unbuckled, and Mary had her shirt off. For a Fat woman, her breasts were tiny, mostly nipple, but the nipples were hard and her hair was tussled and they were both smoking cigarettes. Lance never smoked except after he and Midge made love.

Midge walked into the room and, for a moment, everything was quiet. Everybody just looked at each other.

"Oh my gawd," said Fat Mary. "Oh my gawd."

Midge yelled and grabbed the whiskey bottle and whacked Fat Mary on the side of the head. Fat Mary screamed and grabbed her head. Lance tried to stop his sister, but Midge outweighed him by a good fifty pounds, most of it muscle, from where she had to load those beef carcasses onto the trucks all day. She hit him a roundhouse right to the jaw, and before anything else could happen, ran out of the apartment.

That was the last time Midge and Lance saw each other. After that, Midge left town. She moved to West Virginia for a while and made it as a stripper in a biker bar. She wasn't the prettiest woman they'd ever had dance there, but she had the best moves. Her bump and grind was beyond compare. Every bump, every grind, she thought of Lance. How could he have done that to her? After they'd swam for nine months in the same womb? After they'd lived all those years as man and wife? There was an anger, an outrage in her stripping that really got to the bikers. It was almost spiritual. One time she reduced Gruesome Charlie to tears, and he asked her to marry him. She thought about it for a while, but finally turned him down. The whole scene was getting old, and she was looking for a kind of respectability that the biker life just didn't offer. Still, it was safe, and the money was good. That's when she knew she had to leave West Virginia, before she got sucked into that world forever and had to live in a misery of "what ifs" and "if onlys."

The real kicker, of course, was when she found the Lord. Midge wasn't given over to the dainties and regularities which govern most people's day to day lives and a regular church or standard preacher might never have moved her toward the light. It took a force both greater and lesser than your run of the mill church experience to get Midge's attention. That force, in the form of Cleotis B. Everheart, a sixty-eight-year-old black man with a threadbare gray suit, a black fedora, which he respectfully doffed as he entered the building, one leg, one eye, and a four-day growth of beard, hobbled into the club one bright afternoon and sat down at the edge of the stage, ordered a four dollar beer, and watched Midge dance down to her g-string. Midge noticed Cleotis right away, and not just because he was missing significant portions of his body.

The thing is, most of the guys who came to watch the girls dance were pretty quiet. It was a rare shift when Bobby, the bouncer, had to so much as raise an eyebrow at anybody. Mostly the guys drank their beer and watched the girls and talked to them between their dances, bought them champagne—well, ginger ale, actually, but the guys didn't know the difference and most of them probably wouldn't have cared. Mostly it was kind of sweet. It wasn't that Cleotis was loud or disrespectful, just the opposite. If anything, he was too quiet.

Cleotis visited the club each afternoon for seven afternoons, Monday through Monday week, with Sunday off because the club was closed. He always sat at the edge of the stage and always drank three beers before standing up and lurching out the door and disappearing into the world. The first six times Cleotis visited the club, he never said a word to Midge or any of the other girls, except for the one who came to his table to bring his beer. The only word he said then was, "beer."

The only contact he made with the dancers was the single dollar he tipped whichever girl happened to be dancing when he finished his last beer. Cleotis put the dollar on the edge of the stage, not trying, as did most of the customers, to slip it inside the girl's panties. On all but one of these occasions, Midge was the dancer on stage when Cleotis was ready to leave. That one time, Midge had swapped shifts with Bunny Snodgrass so that Bunny could leave early and go to her daughter's dance recital. "She does the ballet," Bunny always said to anybody who'd listen. So that one time Bunny got Cleotis's dollar, but Midge got the other six. On the seventh day that Cleotis sat in the bar, he finally had something to say.

"You look good," Cleotis said. "They's a part of you that's bad, a part that's fallen, but you look good, and I guess that's better than some." He said this as he was placing his dollar on the stage. The music had just faded out, and the room was quiet as dust in still air, so Midge heard him clearly. There were a half-dozen other men scattered about the room, but no one else apparently heard or cared about what the old man had to say. Midge was supposed to mingle after she finished dancing, and Cleotis had piqued her interest a couple of days before, the way he started coming and going from the bar as if on a schedule. This was the first time he was still in his seat when she finished her act. She got down off of the stage and sat in a chair beside Cleotis.

"Hi," she said. "I'm Midge. What's your name?"

Cleotis nodded his head in a respectful bow. "I am pleased to make your acquaintance," he said, then he told her his name.

"You want to buy me a glass of champagne?" Midge asked. Cleotis smiled the tiniest smile.

"No," he said. "That won't do. I have to stick with my method."

"Your method?"

"Three beers at four dollars apiece and then I leave a dollar. That's thirteen dollars I leave here lighter than when I came in. You know why I leave thirteen dollars lighter every time?"

"Because you're cheap?"

"Because that's what killed Jesus. That's what got him at the Last Supper. They was him and twelve disciples at that table, so old number thirteen was either Him or Judas, depending on how you look at it. Number thirteen was either the Lamb or the goat. That thirteen I give to you gets it off of me. It's a terrible burden being number thirteen. I expect most folks think they'd be Jesus if they had to be the thirteenth at that table, but most wouldn't measure up. They's lots more goats than they is Lambs in this world. I give up old number thirteen, so I don't have to make that choice."

Midge knew she was supposed to hustle up more drinks out of Cleotis, but she was pretty sure he wouldn't spend another dollar on this visit, not after that speech. She was also pretty sure she didn't want to sit here with him, because, most of all, she was pretty sure he was crazy. A religious fanatic at least, maybe something worse. Anyhow, Midge didn't want to be a lamb or a goat, and she didn't want to talk to Cleotis anymore.

"I've got to go," she said. "I've got to get back to work."

"You go on, now. I've got rid of old thirteen, and that's all I need."

Midge felt the dollar against the skin of her hip. She was sure she could feel the very dollar that Cleotis had left at the edge of the stage and she had stuck into the band of her g-string, just like all her tips. She could feel it burning her skin. She reached down and yanked that dollar away and held it in her hand, looking at it. She wanted to give it back to Cleotis, but that just made her feel foolish. A dollar's a dollar and that's all this was, after all. She smoothed it out on the table between them just as Cleotis stood up from the table.

"I don't want to be number thirteen, mister," she said.

"I don't reckon you got much choice, honey," he said. "We's all number thirteen every minute of our lives. I just try to find a way to unburden myself of it, but it don't really do no good."

Cleotis picked up his hat and bowed slightly from the waist; then he turned and, with a certain dignity, clomped out of the club, his real leg then his artificial leg creating a rhythm like a slow heartbeat as he made his way to the door and then, once more, disappeared into the street. Midge took the dollar back from the table and looked at it again. It looked like somebody had used it for a shopping list sometime. The words, "tuna, bulbs, flour, roach spray," were written in a vertical column to the right of President Washington's face. She felt nervous inside, and she wasn't sure whether it was because she believed that Cleotis was crazy, or worse, that she believed he was sane. If he was sane, he might even be holy. There didn't seem to be anything especially holy about a dollar bill with a reminder to pick up a can of roach spray, but still Midge put the dollar aside, didn't spend it like she did the rest of her tips. It was more like a souvenir than anything else, she supposed, a souvenir of an encounter with something that you couldn't quite get to in the normal world, and, for a long time thereafter, she liked to pull it out every now and again and take a look.

The thing is, crazy or not, Cleotis got her to thinking. She knew a thing or two about sin and betrayal. Maybe she deserved what Lance did to her, just from the simple fact of his being her brother and their having relations and all, but Lance was just as guilty as she was about the sex. For him to betray her made him worse than Judas, maybe; the damned betraying the damned. Midge thought about this question quite a bit and the more she thought about it, the more she began to believe that she had a soul and that maybe it was beyond saving and that Lance was surely bound for hell. You'd never catch Midge in a church service, but she became more worried than most about the big questions of faith. She didn't want to be the Lamb or the goat.

Cleotis never came back to the club after the seventh time and Midge was glad of it. He gave her the creeps. In fact, everything about her life was beginning to give her the creeps. She started seeing everybody she knew as number thirteens, potential saviors or betrayers, and it started to wear pretty hard on her nerves. She knew she had to get away, and the only place she could think to go was home.

So she moved back to Columbus. It had been five years since she had left there, and in that time, she had had no communication with Lance. She hoped he was long gone, maybe out west somewhere like he used to talk about. "They've got food stamps in Montana, just the same as here," he always used to say. Lance was like that, always looking for a free ride. Midge, on the other hand, always worked. Ever since they were little, she was the one who was mowing lawns or picking up pop bottles or doing odd jobs for the neighbors for pocket money. When they lived together, Lance stayed home and took care of the house while Midge worked at the slaughterhouse. Now she had to find a job in Columbus, and she didn't want to strip any longer. Her first thought was to go back to the slaughterhouse, but when she applied they turned her down flat. They remembered her down there, and she'd always done a pretty good job, but the way she ran out without even telling anybody she was quitting, the personnel office said they just couldn't take a chance on her. She made the rounds, answered newspaper ads, went to the employment office. Nothing worked. Her savings were thinning and things looked bad. And her eyes were getting worse.

Midge had had bad vision since birth, but in recent years it was getting a lot worse. She saw spots, and the world looked like it existed somewhere just beyond a thin layer of smoke. The doctors told her the problem could probably be corrected with surgery. They gave her an eighty percent chance of 20-20 vision with the proper care. Without the operation she could go blind. But there was no way she could afford to get it done. She had no money, no insurance. She could see well enough to get by, but who knew how things would be in five years? Midge had a good idea about that, but she didn't like to think about it.

She met Jake at a bar. It was after a long day of job hunting and she was tired. She'd already had a few whiskey sours when he came over and sat by her, and in her exhaustion and frustration, fear and bad eyesight, he looked the spitting image of Lance, of the way Lance looked five years ago. She wasn't so far gone that she thought it actually was him, but it was nice to see a face that reminded her of the good times. They sat and talked and Jake bought her a few drinks. They ended up at his place, and for Midge, it was like the clock had turned backward. The sex was wild, great, angry, dangerous, just like the old days. When she climaxed, she yelled out her brother's name, but Jake didn't seem to mind. He just kept right on ramming her with that big thing of his.

Later, when he held her in his arms, she cried and told him about her lost love, how much he looked like Lance, and how awful it had been to come home and find Fat Mary there. She didn't tell Jake that Lance was her brother. They hit it off well, and Midge moved in with Jake. She still went out every day and looked for a job, but had no luck. At night they shook the bed till the springs screamed, and even though Midge desperately wanted a job, both of them were reasonably content.

That was until the day she woke up and her vision was noticeably worse. Instead of smoke, now it was like she was looking through gauze. She knew it was now or never for the operation. Midge told Jake but Jake didn't have that kind of money. After much deliberation, they decided the only way was to hit somewhere and get the money. When Jake suggested the 7-Eleven, Midge said okay. She'd only been there once, ten years earlier, after her grandmother's funeral, so there was no danger of being recognized.

They planned the operation. Midge got out a couple of pairs of pantyhose for them to use as masks. Jake bought each of them a twelve-inch hunting knife at Wal-Mart. He wanted to get a gun, but Midge said no. She didn't like the idea of anybody getting shot. The night before they were set to pull the hold up, they were sitting around Jake's apartment drinking beer. They had made love, and now they were drinking beer and watching television. It was a Tuesday, and the fights were on.

"You like the fights, baby?" he asked.

"Why not?" She didn't really care one way or the other. Most of those guys that fought on TV didn't look like they could last a minute with the guys who used to come into the bar and watch her dance. Once she'd seen Gruesome Charlie take out two college guys at the same time. The college guys knew karate or something, but when they hit Charlie it just seemed to bounce off. When he hit them, they crumbled. Midge didn't care for violence, but when it happened she dealt with it. Like when she found Lance and Fat Mary. The violence was in the air even before she came into the room. She had no more control over that than if Mary had walked over and hit her. Midge snuggled close to Jake and took a drink from her beer. She could barely make out what was on the screen, anyway.

They had tuned in late and the main event was about to begin. It was an over-the-hill former champ against a young bull. Only the bull didn't have much experience, and the smart money was on the former champ. The fight started with the younger man charging in wildly. He had no jab but let fly with a hard right hook. The former champion got out of the way and tagged him twice before shuffling out of range. The fight went on that way for the first round. The young man kept lunging, the older man kept getting out of the way and tagging him.

"Pretty good, huh?" said Jake.

"I guess so."

"He's a pro, baby. That's us tomorrow night. Pros."

The second round started, and the younger fighter lunged across the ring before the former champ quite made it off his stool. He caught the former champ with a hard right to the head and then dug a left into the gut. The younger fighter started raining shots to his opponent's head. He hit him six or seven times before the referee could step between them. The older man slumped to the canvas and didn't move again. They carried him

146

out of the arena on a stretcher, still. Midge and Jake sat there on the couch watching, not saying anything. Then Jake hit the remote and the screen went blank.

They'd decided to hit the 7-Eleven at just after three a.m., because they figured the place would probably be deserted then. Jake drove them over in his old, blue Dodge Charger. He parked at the edge of the lot, where the clerk couldn't see the car. They pulled the pantyhose over their heads, grabbed the knives and went inside.

The place was empty, except for the clerk, a painfully thin woman of about thirty. She was behind the counter, eating a cup of yogurt and drinking a Diet Coke. Lance and Midge went straight for the counter. By the time the clerk looked up, they were standing right in front of the March of Dimes coin box, their knives out and pointed at her.

"All right," said Lance. "This is a stick up. We want all the money." Midge stood beside him, pointing her knife. With the added screen created by the pantyhose, she was functionally blind. She could detect movement and that, with Lance's voice, was enough to guide her to the counter. Even with not being able to make her out, there was something about the clerk that bothered Midge, but she couldn't quite put her finger on it. Then the woman spoke.

"Oh my gawd," she said. "Oh my gawd."

"What did you say?" said Midge. Then to Jake, "Does she have a name tag?"

"Mary," he said. "Her name's Mary."

"Is she Fat?"

"Fat? No, skinny. Okay, Mary, let's have the money." He shook his knife at her, and Mary opened the cash register. She got a bag from under the counter and began shoving the cash register money into it.

"Did you used to be Fat?" Midge demanded. "Did they call you Fat Mary?"

"Oh my gawd," Mary said. Then she said, "Is that you, Midge?"

"Holy Jesus," said Midge. "This is the one," she said to Jake. "This is Fat Mary."

Fat Mary was skinny now, and she was whimpering behind her counter. There was a gun under the counter for situations just like this, but Mary froze. She didn't even think about the gun.

"Don't hurt me, Midge. That stuff with Lance is ancient history. Just take the money and leave." She had all the money in the bag, and she thrust it across the counter toward Jake.

"We gotta take her with us. She knows who I am."

"I thought you said nobody would remember you here!"

Midge swept her arms across the counter, feeling for the money bag.

"Let's go," she said, finding it. "Grab Mary." Jake grabbed Mary by the arm, and the three of them left the store. They put Mary in the back seat, and Jake got them out of there. Jake and Midge pulled the pantyhose off of their heads just as soon as the Charger was out of the parking lot.

Nobody knew what to say. Mary sat in the back seat crying, and Jake was behind the wheel. Midge rode shotgun, eyes straight ahead, body rigid. Without turning around she said, "You bitch." Then she turned. "You fucking bitch." Midge cocked her arm and slapped Mary as hard as she could, right across the mouth.

"Settle down, God damn it," said Jake. "You're gonna make me wreck if you don't settle down." Midge thought about hitting Mary again, but Jake sounded dangerous so she turned back around in her seat and sat there, quiet.

"So, what became of Lance?" she finally said.

"What?"

"Where's Lance?" Her voice was as even as she could make it. "Is he still around?"

Mary rubbed her hand across her cheek. She was whimpering, and for a minute she didn't say anything.

"Lance's in prison," she finally said.

Midge turned around again and squinted at Mary.

"What the hell for?" Mary squirmed in her seat and looked at her hands.

"Remember how much Lance liked to drink? One night when I was working third shift at the morgue, Lance came by to hang out with me. He used to do that sometimes. Sometimes I'd give him money for wine. One night I didn't have any money to give him, and he'd already had a few before he got there. More than a few, really. When I had my back turned he got into one of the lockers and pulled out a bag of..." Mary stopped and looked out the window.

"Bag of what?" Jake said, eyeing her in the rearview.

"Bag of parts."

"Parts?"

"You know, body parts. He slipped out with the bag and they caught him near a liquor store, trying to sell the meat as steak. He's doing a year in the county jail. I got fired, of course."

"Of course," said Jake. "Jesus."

"This guy was the one you were telling me about? Your boyfriend?"

"Boyfriend? Is that what she said?"

"Don't," said Midge. "Don't say a fucking word." She turned to Jake. "Just get us out of here."

Jack drove out of the city, trying to be inconspicuous. He cruised just below the speed limit and didn't so much as run a single yellow light. Five miles out and all that remained of Columbus was the glow of its lights blotting out most of the stars. Fifteen miles later and they might as well have been on the moon. Jake pulled onto a side road, two lanes, with a few scattered businesses, all dark, nobody around to bother them. Midge opened the money bag and brought the cash close to her eyes so she could count their haul.

"There's just eighty-seven bucks in here," she said. "I can't do anything with eighty-seven bucks." Jake slammed the brakes and pulled onto the shoulder. He put his head in his hands and sat there, shaking back and forth.

"What did you do to us, Mary?" he shouted. "You think we're kidding around?"

"It was her brother, is what it was," Mary said. "Lance was Midge's brother. She was doing it with him, too."

"Shut up," said Midge.

"They were a couple of sex perverts," said Mary.

"I don't care if he was her mother," said Jake. "Where's the rest of the money?"

"I'm warning you," said Midge.

"There's no money, I tell you. That's all the money we had in the register. I can't get into the safe and besides, there's not too much in there, either."

Midge thought Mary was awfully self-assured for someone in her position. It didn't seem normal to be so snotty when you were the one who had just been kidnapped at knife-point. Midge decided to bring Mary down a peg.

"You sure were fat," Midge said. "You were about the fattest woman I ever saw."

Mary's chin quivered. She blinked twice and then the tears came.

"But I got better," she whispered. "I'm pretty now. Prettier than you." Then, yelling, "You bitch!"

"Okay," Jake said. "Everybody out of the car." He glanced out the windows, then opened his door and stepped onto the shoulder. He left the engine running.

Midge wasn't too sure about this, but she did it anyway, grabbing a handful of Mary's hair and pulling her out of the car. There was a tall maple tree just off the road, its late autumn leaves half gone. Jake made Mary sit down beside it.

"You move, you're dead."

"Oh my gawd." Mary was crying now, choking out the words through wracking sobs, repeating the phrase like a chant.

Jake walked behind Mary, and Midge followed him. He held up his knife for Midge to see and pantomimed a downward thrust in the direction of Mary's neck. Midge felt a strong urge to vomit, but managed not to do it. She was conflicted. Mary getting dead might solve some problems in the short run, and it would sure be a solid revenge for her stealing Lance. But still.

"No," she said, low enough for Mary not to hear.

"Yes," he said. "No choice."

Jake raised the knife, stiff armed, over his head. He brought it down fast, but before the point touched Mary he came up short, hobbled by a blinding pain just below his floating rib and deep into his gut. Midge released the handle of her knife and backed off, her blade stuck to the hilt in Jake's body.

"Oh, Fuck," Jake screamed, grabbing at the knife handle, trying to pull it out of him. "Oh, Fuck, oh Fuck, oh Fuck!" Jake's knees buckled, and he fell into the dirt. Mary turned around and saw Jake on the ground, Midge crouched beside him.

"What the fuck, Midge? Why did you do this to me?" Jake was curled up, blood pooling quickly onto the ground beside him.

Midge wondered, too. Everything had happened so fast, and there had been no time to think. She saw Jake a half second away from killing Mary, and she stopped him. It puzzled her for a second, and then she knew.

"I didn't want you to go to hell," she said.

"What?"

"My eyes aren't worth you going to hell. We didn't start out to kill anybody, and I couldn't let you put that on your soul."

"Are you shitting me? You fucking gutted me, Midge. You fucking killed me. You go to hell, you crazy bitch."

"Baby, I was damned already. I'm so sorry, so sorry, so sorry." Her voice trailed off. Jake didn't talk anymore after that. He screamed and grunted and moaned, but along with writhing around some, that was about it. After a while, Jake lost consciousness. Midge raised his head and put it in her lap, stroking his hair and sobbing. A while later, Midge thought of

Mary. She looked toward the tree where Jake had Mary sit, but Mary wasn't there. Then, Midge realized the car was gone, too. Midge didn't budge. She still sat there cradling Jake's head when the police arrived, paced by an ambulance.

Midge didn't want a trial. The court gave her a public defender, a young woman in gray tweed, with short brown hair and a vertical scar traversing her upper lip where, sometime long ago, she'd had a cleft palate repaired, Midge told her she wanted to plead guilty to the charges the police had read to her: armed robbery, kidnapping, and attempted murder. Fortunately for them both, Jake survived the gutting and was released to jail after ten days in intensive care. After a few days of back and forth between Midge's lawyer and the prosecutor, Midge accepted a take it or leave it offer of two ten year sentences to be served concurrently. Jake took his chances at trial, where he blamed, without much success, the whole thing on Midge. His sentence was fifteen years. When they led him from the courtroom, he was still cursing Midge.

She was out in three years, thanks to a combination of good behavior and near total blindness. She learned Braille in prison and, when she was freed, settled for a while in a halfway house before moving to the projects where she survived on food stamps and social security.

Midge sat in her living room one exceptionally hot Saturday morning listening to the oldies channel on the radio and drinking a glass of ice water. Some half-remembered Steppenwolf song had just begun when she heard a knock at the door. Jail and blindness had aged her, so it took her a minute to get to the door and pull it open.

"Yes?"

There was no answer, but Midge knew someone was there. She heard a short, quick gasp, then breathing. Midge was in no mood to get mugged, so she slammed the door as quickly as she could and fumbled the lock shut. A moment later, whoever was out there pounded on the door, then yelled her name.

"Midge? Midge Spivey? Is that you, Midge?"

It had been many years, but Midge knew that voice, was sure of it.

"Lance?"

"Yes, Lance. It's Lance, Midge. It's me. Open the door." She opened it a crack.

"May I come in?"

"I don't know, Lance. It's been a long time. A long time. How did you find me?"

"This is nothing but an accident, Midge. I come to these apartments every few months to witness to people."

"You what?"

"I'm a Christian, Midge. I had a hard go of it for a long time after you left. Drugs, booze, even jail. I can't change our sins, Midge, but I found the Lord three years ago and was called to witness."

Midge took a half step back and opened the door wider. She didn't invite him in, but she didn't tell him to stay outside, either. She sat back down on her couch.

"I'm coming in."

Lance took a seat across from the couch.

"Have you found the Lord?" he asked.

"After all this time, that's what you want to ask me? Can you see that I'm fucking blind? Maybe you could ask me about that?"

"You were a whore, Midge, and I was a whore monger. And a pervert. We were both perverts. I think your soul is more important than your vision. Anyway, I know all about you. All about the robbing and kidnapping and almost murder, even. My wife tells me everything."

"Wife?"

"You might remember Mary. She used to be heavy. We got married a year ago in April. You know what, Midge? Mary forgives you. I forgive you, too. Jesus will forgive you if you ask him. Have you found the Lord?"

Midge heard something in Lance's voice that didn't sound forgiving. More like somebody who thought he was hot shit thinking about throwing cold piss into her face.

"No, Lance. I never found Jesus. I used to think I found Him, but that was wrong. I think maybe he found me, once. I'm not sure, but I think maybe so." She reached for her purse on the coffee table and opened it, rifling through the contents until she found a small coin purse, which she removed and held out to Lance. There was a gun in there too, a .22 caliber pistol, because a woman can't be too careful.

"Take this. I want you to have it."

Lance took the coin purse and opened it. He stuck his fingers inside and pulled out a dollar bill, the only thing that was in there. The dollar was folded into a small rectangle.

"I'm not looking for donations, Midge."

"That's not what this is."

Lance unfolded the dollar and saw there was writing on the front, near Washington's face: "Tuna, bulbs, flour, roach spray."

"Thanks," he said. "I guess."

"I'm a goat, Lance. I wish I were a Lamb, but I'm not. You, I think, are a fucking asshole. Maybe this dollar can help you try to at least climb up to be a goat yourself."

Lance sat there for a moment, his eyes shifting from Midge to the dollar and back.

"I'll pray for you," he finally said. Then he stood to leave.

"You do that, and I will hunt you down and cut your nuts off."

"You're crazy. Jesus doesn't really want you at all."

"Just go, Lance."

"I'll go. And you know what? I'll keep your fucking dollar."

Lance rose quickly and left the apartment, slamming the door behind him. Midge wondered if she should have taken the pistol out of her purse instead of the dollar. Maybe Lance could use a good shooting. Too late now.

154

"Fucking asshole," she said again. She turned her attention back to the radio. Midge felt light, lighter than she had in years. She stood and danced, a good, lusty bump and grind. She kept going, every so often removing an item of clothing and tossing it to the floor, even her panties until, at last, she stood there more naked than she had ever been as a stripper, as naked as a person could be. She found her glass and tipped the ice water over her head. Oh, it felt fine.

"Praise the Lord." she said out loud. "Why not praise his fucking name?"

Rescuing Jessica

So Curtis asked me to go with him to Lexington to get his kid, and I said, "Sure, no big deal." I'd met Jessica a couple of times, and she was well-behaved and sweet for a two year old. I guess you couldn't say the same for her mother. Ever since Belinda and Curt split up, everything had been nasty between them, and Curtis went around mad most of the time. But it was pretty obvious it wasn't so much that she left him that bothered Curtis, but that she left him for a black man and they were living in sin right there with his daughter, just two hours down the Mountain Parkway. Still, I thought this was all no big deal, until we made it past Stanton, and Curt pulled the gun out from under his seat.

There was a fifth of bourbon whiskey in the seat between us, and Curtis had been taking slugs from it every now and again. He was chain smoking Luckies, same as always. The car was littered with empty Lucky Strike packs, and there was an unopened carton in the back seat. Curt smoked each cigarette about half-way down, then flicked it out the window. Then he'd light up another. It was a nervous habit, something he'd been doing the twenty or so years I'd known him. I never saw him put out a smoke, or smoke one all the way down, either. He was going at the bottle pretty good and wanting me to drink, too.

"Come on, man, take a swig." It was the sixth or seventh time he'd offered me the bottle, so I took a swallow just to shut him up. He seemed bent on finishing the bottle, and I figured the more I drank, the less there would be for Curtis. I have no problem with anybody enjoying a drink, but Curtis isn't the world's greatest driver sober, and it worried me some that he was mad and drunk and driving. We used to drink together a lot when I was younger, but ever since I started working out, I've really cut back on the booze.

That's why I was there, anyway. Curt brought me along for intimidation. I've studied karate for about five years, and Curtis has always seemed to think that's a big deal. It was my job to stand around and make sure Melvin, the black dude, didn't get any funny ideas about keeping Jessica away from her daddy. That was okay. From what I knew about Melvin he was a pussy anyway. He was a little guy, a warm-up jock at Keeneland, and soaking wet he couldn't weigh over a hundred pounds. It seemed a little strange to me that Curtis would even feel the need for backup with this midget, but Curt's my long-time buddy, so I didn't give him a hard time about it. But I didn't like the pistol.

"What is that?" I said when he flashed the piece. "What do you intend to do with that thing?"

Curtis had been close mouthed the whole trip, mad as shit, ready to go in and get the little girl. His red hair was tufted and wild on his forehead, and with that ruddy complexion flaming, his face looked like the devil's.

"I'm going to get Jessica away from that whore and her little colored man. You got a problem with that?"

"And you need a piece to keep Melvin from whacking you? Is that it? Jesus, Curtis, get a clue. There's no problem here.

"Damn right there's no problem." He nodded his head and twisted the gun around, feeling its weight. It was a .357 magnum and looked like a real monster in his hand. Curtis smiled and put the gun in the seat between us. He took one last drag on a half-smoked Lucky and tossed it out the window. Thirty seconds later he was fumbling around to light another one.

It was a clear, beautiful day, and I watched billowy white clouds hanging in a sky as blue a sky as I'd ever seen. This was early October, and the leaves were just beginning to turn. I watched as the freshly orange and red and yellow hills got smaller and flatter the closer we got to Lexington. Curtis didn't like to listen to the radio when he was driving, and he didn't much seem to want to talk, so it looked like it would be this way all the way in, me admiring the scenery and Curtis driving and frowning, drinking, smoking his Luckies, and that gun just lying there in the seat. I had the window open and my arm hanging out, and the air, which was getting crisp, felt great.

We hit that lonesome stretch between Salyersville and Slade. This has always been my favorite part of the drive. It's exhilarating, the way the road curves and dips and shoots around between the hills. The trees overhang the pavement there and, when there's no other traffic, it's almost like you've gone back to some other time before you even could see another car come zooming around a bend. You're still forty minutes from where the parkway goes to four-lane, and there's usually not much traffic, so it's a good place to collect your thoughts. Curt and me and some of the boys we went to school with used to drive up there every now and again to explore when we were kids. You can park along the side of the road and jump the guard rail, climb up past the trees and find places, caves and hollows, streams, spots to hang in. We went up there to smoke and drink and lie about girls we wanted to bang.

Even back in high school it was always Belinda this, Belinda that with Curt. They dated all through school and got married a couple of years after graduation. Curtis was working for the newspaper by then, running the press and helping with circulation. They bought a little house over in Abbot and settled in. After about a year they had their first baby, Georgie. Curtis was crazy about that boy, always taking him into town and showing him off. He bought Georgie a basketball and set up a goal beside the house. Of course the boy was too young, but Curtis didn't want to waste any time. Curtis had played ball in school and was the reserve point guard on the last regional championship team ever at Prestonsburg High School. He wanted Georgie to do better.

When he was three, Georgie was in the back yard playing with that basketball, and he got bitten by a copperhead. He hung on for almost a week before he died. Georgie's dying almost killed Curtis and Belinda. Curtis started drinking heavily, and Belinda practically disappeared from sight. Not that she was ever a social butterfly, but Belinda had at least been civil when she ran into anybody at the grocery or on the street. She'd worked as a teller at the First Commonwealth Bank ever since graduation. After Georgie died, she quit her job and, as far as most of us knew, stayed at home. Georgie had been gone almost four years when Jessica was born.

With the new baby, Curt went around all proud and happy for a year or so; then I didn't see much of him. When I did run into him, he didn't look too joyful. It turns out that he found Belinda was sneaking around on him. Not too long after Jessica was born, Belinda went to visit her sister in Lexington. They went to the bar at the Executive Inn to have a few drinks, and that's where she met Melvin. God knows why she got the hots for this tiny little black man, but she did and pretty soon she was visiting her sister about every other week. Curtis became suspicious after a little bit and got onto her about it, and finally Belinda confessed everything. He threw her out and she moved into Melvin's place in Lexington and took Jessica with her. That was about six months ago, and now Curtis was going to get his little girl back.

We'd just gone around a bend and were coming up on a downgrade when we saw Bobby Bruce hitchhiking. Bobby's this mildly retarded black man, about fifty years old, a town character from Prestonsburg who, as long as I remember, got around on his thumb. Sometimes he'd bum money for cigarettes or a Coke when he got a ride, but it wasn't like he was a pest, really, just one of those folks like lots of small towns have, somebody not quite right that everybody kind of watches out for but doesn't think too much about. He had on old, raggedy clothes, like always, overalls and a green work shirt, and his blue and white Kentucky Wildcats cap. He always wore that cap, rain or shine.

It was kind of a surprise to see Bobby on the parkway because you don't see many hitchhikers on that road. For one thing, signs say that it's illegal. For another, there aren't too many places for a hitchhiker to get on the parkway, unless he's traveling from, say, Prestonsburg to Lexington. Also, I had never seen Bobby outside the Prestonsburg city limits. It was the first time I'd ever even considered the idea of Bobby outside of town.

Curtis saw Bobby at the same time I did. He put on his signal when we were almost to him and pulled the car to a stop about a hundred feet up the road. Bobby trotted toward the car, and Curt looked over at me and smiled.

"Watch this," he said. Bobby was almost even with the car when Curtis picked up the gun. Curt rolled down his window and motioned him over. Bobby walked on up.

"Lookin' for a ride?"

"Yes, sure am." He looked like he was about to reach for the door. Curtis flicked a Lucky out the window. He held up the gun and pointed it at Bobby's face. Bobby straightened and took in a deep breath.

"Not looking for no trouble now, no trouble." He backed away slowly, and Curtis pulled the hammer back on his pistol. The gun looked huge in his hand. He moved it a little and it glinted in the sun.

"Come on, man, cut the shit," I whispered. "You don't need to mess with Bobby." Curt flashed me a grin.

"Get the fuck out of here, dummy." Curtis spat out the window. "Today's your lucky day." Bobby stumbled backward and fell down. Curtis laughed and threw the car in gear and took off. He let out a whoop and laughed big in his belly.

"Did you see the look on his face? I bet he shit his britches." It took Curt a full minute to calm down. He noticed I wasn't laughing, and he gave me the evil eye.

"Just practicing," he said, grabbing a cigarette from the pack in his shirt pocket. "Hey, did you see where I put my lighter?" He found it in the seat and fired up another smoke.

I'd known Bobby all my life. When I was little I used to hang out at the Fountain Korner and drink Cokes and read comic books. Bobby was there all the time. Sometimes the girl behind the counter gave him free pop, and I can remember customers buying him hamburgers or french fries if he'd sing for them.

For some reason, the men who loafed around the Fountain Korner always used to get Bobby to sing "Rudolph the Red Nosed Reindeer." The singing was awful, but people had him do it because they thought it was funny. Bobby probably didn't realize how bad he was being fucked with, but I never saw anybody welsh on him. If somebody promised him a hamburger for singing, he always got the burger.

We both had our windows open, and Curtis had the Dodge cruising pretty fast. The air shot in the windows and blew my hair straight back. I needed the air. After that scene with Bobby I wouldn't have been able to breathe right, just me and Curtis, closed up behind glass.

We drove a while, and the day didn't seem as pretty as it had before.

"I wish you hadn't done that stuff to Bobby," I said after a while.

"Oh, Bobby don't mind. If that's the worst thing that ever happens to him, he'll be all right."

Curtis took a big drink of Turkey, shivered and had another. He rolled the lid back on and didn't ask me to drink with him.

"You know," he said, "I've always treated niggers just like they were anybody else. Back in school, nobody gave Jimmy Osborne a chance, but I did." Jimmy was a backup forward on the P-burg basketball team. He and Curtis used to warm the bench together. Jimmy was the first black kid in school and most everybody hated him. He and Curt palled around a little in school, and it's true, I never heard him say one bad word about Jimmy.

161

"But it sure leaves a bad taste in your mouth when your wife runs off with one of 'em. Know what I mean?"

"I guess so."

"Guess so, hell. Shit, man, I loved that woman." Curtis took a big drag on his smoke. "Well, what the fuck. I just want my little girl back. Then all the brothers in the world can take turns with Belinda, and I'll stand back and cheer them on."

A few miles down the road we rounded a tight curve. Curtis was fumbling around for his lighter in the seat, and not paying too much attention to the road. He found the lighter just as we were into the curve, but he hadn't been paying enough attention to what he was doing, and now he had the car a few inches over the yellow line. Ordinarily this would be no big deal because the Parkway is always dead, but today there was a station wagon turning the same curve as us at the same moment. It was a big, green, tuna boat of a car and as we came upon each other, I saw clearly that there was an old guy driving and in the passenger seat was a young girl. I could see that she was pretty, a dark haired girl with a thin face and big eyes. The old guy in the wagon swerved to miss us and lost control. He fishtailed and skidded thirty feet or so, then smashed hard into the rock face of a hill.

Curtis mashed the brake. "Holy Jesus," he said. "Mother fuck."

We pulled off the road, and Curtis took a second to light his cigarette, then we hurried on over to the car. It was like a scene from a bad movie, or one of those films they show in high school to keep kids from driving drunk. Somehow there was gas leaking, and the girl was obviously dead. Her head had gone through the windshield and was lying at a funny angle, twisted halfway around on her neck. Her hair was long, longer than it had looked when we passed each other. Much of her body lay outside the car, and her cheek rested near the center of the hood. The man was in awful shape, but it looked like he might make it. His right leg was caught where the dash had crushed in against the front seat, and he was bleeding pretty good from the face. His left eye was gouged and bloody and he was screaming.

We tried to pull him out, but he was wedged in too tight. Every time we tried to move him he screamed harder. Curtis had that Lucky in his mouth, like always, and in the excitement, I guess he just didn't think. He took a last drag and threw it on the ground. There was gas there, but it hadn't seemed like too much. Still, it caught up pretty quick and then there was fire everywhere. The young girl just lay there and the old guy twisted around yelling and trying to get out and not having any luck.

"God damn it," I said. "You stupid asshole." There was nothing to do. He was stuck in there and the car was burning up. "We can't let this happen," I said. "What the hell are we going to do?" I ran over to the car again and tried to pull the old guy out, but the fire was too much. I had him by the arm, trying one last time to pull him out and he was cussing me and crying. I started crying too and cussing back, but there was nothing I could do.

"Get the hell out of there," Curtis yelled. "Get away." The flames shot higher and I backed off. The old man's clothes were starting to catch fire. I could only see part of the girl's body, but I could smell her hair burning. The smell was all mixed in with the gasoline smell and the black smoke, but I could smell the hair for certain.

Curtis stood his ground for a second, then went over to the car and came back. He had his gun in his hand. "Do you want to do it, or should I?"

"Do what?"

"Kill that poor son of a bitch. We can't let him burn to death."

"You're crazy." His eyes were big and wild and his skin was as red as fire. The old man must have seen the gun because his screams turned into "Oh God Oh God Oh my Jesus.

Curtis walked to about three feet away from the vehicle. He pointed the gun at the man and stood there. His arm was halfway extended, and as he stood there I saw his hand shaking. The fire reflected in the nickel plating and it jerked and jumped with his shaking. The old guy in the car was still yelling, but he wasn't looking at Curtis or me anymore. He was yelling down toward his right shoulder, twisting, like he was scrunching his body away from the gun. Curtis froze. The fire was everywhere and I was afraid the car would explode. I didn't want anybody to shoot the guy, but he was burning.

I yelled for Curtis to give me the gun, but he didn't answer. I yelled again and thought about tackling him, but five years of karate, a hundred years, is no match for a .357.

"Curtis, give me the gun." I said it quietly. My voice seemed to be coming from somewhere else. He looked at me and at first it didn't seem like he would hand over the gun, then he let his arm drop and he gave it to me. The driver was burning. I couldn't even see if he was still alive, but if he was, he was in agony. Nobody should die that way. I aimed the gun, squared up and fired. It sounded like a cannon going off. The old guy jerked back as the slug hit him and then he was quiet. I bent over and vomited. The car was burning and as soon as I could straighten up, we walked fast back to our car, got in and drove.

Curtis was shaking. "He was going to die, man. And he was going to burn to death. We couldn't get him out. No way." He banged his fist on the dash and gunned the engine. I picked up the whiskey and had a big drink. It felt like fire in my throat. I almost vomited again but held it back and then took another drink.

We were a mile or so down the road when Curtis remembered Bobby Bruce. "Son of a bitch," he said. "I showed him my gun." Curtis pulled off the road and turned the car around. We sped back the way we'd come. My heart was beating hard and fast. Curtis punched a rhythm into the door with his left hand as he drove with his right. We were driving fast, whipping around curves and rocketing down the straight stretches.

"What if he got a ride, man? What if he hears about that old man being shot and tells somebody about us? Jesus." Curtis was well into panic, and he kept his eyes turned fast to the road, looking for Bobby.

The quality of light was becoming softer. Air shot into the car and it felt like ice. The trees held fast to the mountains and the sides of the road like enormous red hands. I could still smell the gasoline and the burning hair. We hit a long straight stretch and off in the distance I saw a figure walking along the side of the road. Curtis slowed the car. He held the gun in his lap and I looked down and saw that it was shaking in his hand.

"God damn it," Curtis said, his eyes fixed straight forward. "All I wanted was to raise my own baby. Now look at what's happened to me."

We weren't speeding now, and the figure was slowly getting larger. It was icy in the car. I couldn't remember if Curt ever hung out at the Fountain Korner. Did he ever hear Bobby sing? Curtis was holding the gun a little higher, up by his belly. It was now clearly Bobby ahead of us and there was a buzzing in my ears. The day became bright, crystalline. We pulled just in front of Bobby and he stood there looking at us. I couldn't tell if he was afraid or not. Bobby was a lot bigger than Melvin, the colored man Belinda and Jessica were living with, but he didn't look any more dangerous than a puppy.

"We've got to rescue Jessica, man," I whispered to Curtis. He looked over at me. The buzzing in my ears was enormous. Curtis looked over at me and he was sweating hard in the cold afternoon. He had his gun in his lap and Bobby Bruce stood twenty feet away from us and the Parkway was deserted and the day was as bright and lovely as any I can remember. Curtis stuck his head out the window.

"I'm sorry about that before, Bobby," he said. "You need a ride? Come on over here and sing us a song. We'll take you anywhere you need." The day was spinning and spinning as Bobby stood there regarding us. Curtis fired up a Lucky and my mind fell back through clear air toward deserted caves and hollows, generally traveling away from a plume of smoke building up in the west.

Castaway

You're sitting in your living room, minding your own business. *Gilligan's Island* is on the TV, the episode where the Mosquitoes come to the island but don't rescue the castaways because they see Mary Ann and Ginger and Mrs. Howell put on a show that's meant to impress them, but what it really does is show them they don't need the competition. The Mosquitoes split in the middle of the night, but leave an autographed album as a gift. If you look closely, you can tell it's just an empty album cover, the way it bends in Gilligan's hands.

There's a knock at the door. You are neither excited nor disappointed at the prospect of company. Not even puzzled. You get up from the couch and answer the door.

It's a man you've never seen before, standing there in the hall. Hello, he says. Have you talked with Jesus today?

No, you say. Not as far as I know. The man smiles. A little joke. May he come in? May he come in and talk with you? Just a few minutes of your time?

You hesitate for a moment. *The Wild, Wild West* is coming on next, but you've seen every episode a million times. Okay, you tell him. Sure, come on in.

You sit down on the couch and the man takes the easy chair. You mute the TV with the remote control.

Nice place you got, he says. Wonderful, really.

Thanks, you say. Can I get you something? Cup of coffee?

That would be nice.

You go to the kitchen and whip up some instant Folgers. When you get back, the man is standing by your bookcase. There's a picture of Marjorie in a small frame, right in front of *The Sound and the Fury*, a book you were supposed to read in college but never got around to.

Pretty girl, he says.

Yes, she is.

Girlfriend?

Sister.

She's very pretty, he says again.

Yes. Thank you.

You sit down on the couch, and he takes the easy chair again.

Do you know the Lord? he asks.

I don't know. It's been a long time since I've been to church, since I was a kid. I haven't been to church since my grandmother's funeral when I was twelve years old.

That's a long time.

Yes.

You don't know what to expect. You're feeling stupid for letting him into your apartment. Right now you could be watching James West matching wits with Dr. Ocularis, instead of feeling uncomfortable talking about Jesus with a stranger.

I didn't catch your name, you say.

I'm Frank Burton, he says. I'm with the Lord. And your name is?

Spivey, Bill Spivey.

I'm glad to meet you, Mr. Spivey. Jesus would be happy to have your heart open to him.

You sit there looking at him.

Jesus loves you, you know.

You smile a little and try to think of something to say but nothing happens.

Won't you let Him into your heart, Mr. Spivey? Won't you open your heart to the Lord?

168

You take a sip of coffee, but what you want is a beer. You look over at the picture of Marjorie. She's still missing, three years after she went to the mall to buy a pair of shoes. She went to get new shoes and was never seen again.

I want to be open, you say.

Praise God, he says.

I want to be.

Will you pray with me, brother?

You think about Marjorie and those shoes. There were all sorts of theories, and most of them ended with her dead, an awful death at the hands of a lunatic. In truth, though, the police are still baffled.

Frank gets down on his knees in front of the couch. He holds his hands out toward you. You feel stupid, but you do it. You get down there with him. Frank starts praying in a loud voice, and you wish he would hurry, finish up. After a while, he does. After he says amen, you mutter it, too.

Praise Jesus, brother, he says. Frank takes a small, green Bible out of his pocket and puts it in your hand. Then he walks toward the door.

Goodbye, you say. Goodbye, Frank. He waves his hand and steps into the hall and walks away.

She was only twenty years old. Your little sister.

You walk back into the living room and take her picture and stare at her face. There are so many questions.

On television, Artemus Gordon is in one of his disguises that every viewer sees through immediately, but none of the villains ever do. Sometimes even James West is fooled. He's dressed like a pirate, complete with a parrot on his shoulder, an eye patch and a wooden leg. It's really ingenious how they got the wooden leg to look real.

You go into the kitchen and get that beer, then plop back on the couch, still holding Marjorie's picture. You don't want to cry, but you can't help it. Maybe later you'll call your folks. Now you sit in front of the television and stare, just like anyone would.

169

When Giraffes Flew

After the giraffes acquired flight, all bets were off. They were silent fliers, not even the beating of wings, of course, as giraffes are not so equipped. They flew by some other mechanism no one understood and were impressively efficient, considering the evolutionary path their species had heretofore trod. The more mysterious of them hid among the clouds, rarely appearing within sight of man.

The young were more of a nuisance. Their trajectories were often decidedly terrestrial, and it was common to see them soaring overhead in majestic herds, like human teenagers cruising the main drag after dark, except the giraffes didn't seem to care if it were day or night. You might as soon catch them up there at dawn or noon as midnight. When they expelled their waste, that was a problem. A booming industry in broad-brimmed hat and helmet manufacture and sales sprung up quickly to feed a panicked demand. Municipalities hired more and better sanitation crews to keep the dung and urine on the streets to a minimum. The tops of houses and other structures were more of a problem and, for the most part, owners were expected to maintain them at their own expense. Most people were good about this, especially after the first few roofs collapsed under the accumulating weight.

An even bigger problem was the giraffes' habit of snatching people away. This began after folks fell into acceptance of the new, flying-giraffe reality. When people no longer gazed obsessively skyward to watch them, giraffes enjoyed a stealthy existence of silent flight and human disregard. Maybe they became bored, or maybe giraffes had a mean streak no one had picked up on before. Whatever the reason, one day, the giraffes began swooping down and grabbing people in their four legs, more or less in the same fashion as those arcade games where, for a few quarters, the player moves a claw inside a Plexiglas box and tries to snatch a ball or plush toy. While humans who actually have the skill to win such prizes are rare, the giraffes were almost one hundred percent accurate. They mostly went for small people —kids and the shrunken elderly.

It seemed inevitable that giraffes would drop their victims from a great altitude, making of them people bombs and fomenting terror on a scale previously unconsidered. One imagined a mother, perhaps, being flattened by the hurtling body of a baby she had, only days previous, suckled at her breast. Or lovers' lanes wiped out by an inundation of geriatrics, the grandparents of young lovers crashing down on automobile hoods, breaking windshields and so forth. People worried.

But none of that happened. The taken never returned. The brightest minds held a conference to determine where the missing might be. Some thought the giraffes were eating them, but others pointed out that there was no case of giraffes eating people in the historical record and, besides, giraffes were herbivores. The counter to that line of thought was that, until recently, they didn't fly, either, but there was still the question of what became of the bones. Since no one was willing to believe that giraffes would consume every part of a human being, right down to the marrow, the consumption theory lost traction.

It eventually came to pass that people decided the young giraffes were delivering their catches to the older giraffes who hid among the clouds. The purpose could not be known to full certainty, but over time an entire belief system grew up around the missing people frolicking in the sky with their new giraffe families. These children and old people, it was decided, were learning the ways of the giraffe and one bright day might return filled with radiant splendor to show the earthbound the way to glory.

But the wonders of the world never last, and so it was with the giraffes. After only a few generations, the giraffes stopped taking people and not long after that, they, too, disappeared from the skies. The giraffes did not return to Earth, but simply vanished, as though they had never been more than a lovely notion.

People wrote books about the giraffes and the ascended missing and gathered in regular meetings to silently send good wishes to them all. Priests eventually took charge, and a spirit of grace filled all who congregated. As the years passed, the people who knew the missing began dying off, as did those who had seen the giraffes in flight. Eventually, people decided that giraffes had never flown, had never taken young children or old people away. And not so very long after that, it became fashionable to say there never were any giraffes in the first place, not even the kind who walked the Earth. Who is to say this is wrong?

About the Author

Jeff Weddle grew up in Prestonsburg, a small town in the hill country of Eastern Kentucky. He has worked as a public library director, disc jockey, newspaper reporter, movie projectionist, Tae Kwon Do teacher, and fry cook, among other things.

His first book, *Bohemian New Orleans: The Story of the Outsider and Loujon Press* (University Press of Mississippi, 2007), won the Eudora Welty Prize and helped inspire Wayne Ewing's documentary, *The Outsiders of New Orleans: Loujon Press* (Wayne Ewing Films, 2007), for which Weddle served as associate producer. Other books include *Betray the Invisible* (OEOCO, 2010) and, as co-author, *The Librarian's Guide to Negotiation: Winning Strategies for the Digital Age* (Information Today, 2012).

Weddle is an associate professor in the School of Library and Information Studies at the University of Alabama.

.

www.ingramcontent.com/pod-product-compliance
Lightning Source LLC
Chambersburg PA
CBHW021011180626
46814CB00003B/1246